Corporate America

Refreshing the Christian Businessman

By

Michael Reagan

xulon PRESS

Contents

Preface

A little Back Round

"Teach me to do your will, for you are my God;
may your good Spirit lead me on level ground".
Psalm 143:10

First off I just want to say that I am writing this to glorify
God's name. That is my sole purpose; it is not for my
glory but for His. Right off the bat, I just want to say that I
am not the best writer by any stretch of the imagination. So I
hope that you can overlook any grammar and sentence struc-
ture errors. I pray and believe that this will take a fresh look
for businessmen and women who are Christians. I know that
it is very easy to get into a routine and to forget our roots and
values sometimes. We have so many goals and so many
different people that we have to worry about, customers, co-
workers, families, deadlines, and what's for dinner. The list
of things that we need to do just goes on and on. What I have
done is take some parallels of the business world and tried to
tie them into a Christian perspective. Hopefully this will help

us to refocus on what we are really here on earth to do, which is to live for Christ.

Also I hope for anyone that picks this book up that might not be a Christian, someone that is not living his or her life for Christ. That you may come to know Jesus Christ through this book. This is for those people who are looking for something more than just the stress of running a company and meeting their goals at the end of the quarter.

I gave my life to Christ when I was 13. However it was a convenient faith, when things were easy and when family and friends were doing it I was. However at college my personal faith really took off. I was able to understand that Jesus wanted a personal relationship with me. My relationship with Christ became like a relationship with my best friend. Looking back on how everything happened I know God has a plan for my life. I am not exactly sure what that is. I just have to trust Him daily and he will take care of me. I graduated with a Bachelor's of Science in Finance. I believe that God called me to the business world, at least for a period of time. He had provided an opportunity at a community bank. It was a trainee position where I would rotate around the bank, throughout all of the different departments. Which allowed me to gain a lot of experience in a short amount of time. In addition to the experience, it allowed me to see all of the ins and outs of the bank. It also allowed me to meet and work with a bunch of different people and personality types. Which God really blessed me through this rotation at the bank on both a professional level and a personal level.

I believe that God has big plans for both you and myself. I am a firm believer that Christians can enter in to the secular work force and make a difference for Christ in the workplace. That God doesn't call us all to be Preachers or missionaries. I believe that I am a missionary to the people at my workplace. I am supposed to set an example for my co-workers and customers, and hopefully they will be able to see something different in my life. And that will cause conversations that will enable to me talk about Christ and my relationship with Him. I am sure that we would all agree that living as a Christian not always easy. In fact I believe God holds us to a higher standard. Let's keep in mind that we will be rewarded for everything that we do.

Now I don't know everything, not even close. And that goes for Christianity and the business world both. I have not been out of school all that long, but I believe that God laid this on my heart to write this. And He has opened my eyes up since I have entered the work force. As for me being a Christian I have my ups and downs. I am just trying to constantly search after God every day. And I once again pray that with these words that I write He will be pleased with and it will honor Him. I encourage you if you can, make marks throughout this book. I have found that it has helped. Maybe I have found a passage that has really encouraged me. So I mark it and from time to time I will just flip through old books that I have read and it will stick out at me. Or maybe there is something that makes no sense that you have a question about it, mark it. Hopefully your question might be answered later on in the book or you can ask someone. And if nothing else it helps keep us focused.

Once again thank you for choosing this book. I hope that you are able to grow in your faith and your relationship with Christ. I hope you will welcome the challenges. Its through our willingness to change, that is how God uses us and changes people around us. It is amazing what God can do if we let him.

It's all about
the Money

"Even now the reaper draws his wages, even now he harvests the crop for eternal life, so that the sower and the reaper may be glad together".
John 4:36

First, the reason why most of us are in the business world, it's all about the money. Well being in business of course is all about making money. You have entrepreneurs that come up with ideas and are willing to take risks and open up business. But those entrepreneurs need people to sell their services to the business the entrepreneurs are starting. And we as employees, we do sell our services to our companies for what we think we are worth or what can we get. And we base this on all kinds of things. We compare ourselves to others, as well as our education level if we have a masters or a bachelor's or even just a high school diploma. Our responsibilities also play a role on deciding on how much we should receive for our services. The number of hours, the type of skills we need, traveling, and so on all plays a role.

A lot of people get caught up chasing after the almighty dollar. However most people never catch it. No matter how much you are making it will never be enough. "The Americans have little faith. They rely on the power of the dollar," Ralph Waldo Emerson[i]. We always want more and more, or that new car or that new house. And people just get caught up in this mess. They are in competition with their neighbors and friends for the newer cars and the bigger houses.

I worked in the trades as I was going through college. It was a pretty good paying job, especially for a college kid. I usually was able to work as many hours as I wanted to, which sometimes was ten hour days, six or seven days a week. But as I am working all of these hours and am having conversation with these guys I am working with. It was awful just hearing how they were having problems with their wife and their kids were not listening to them. Some you would ask them how their children were doing and they would have to stop and think for a little bit, and then they would just come back with a simple answer "okay." Sometimes when my co-workers were home they would complain that all their kids did was play Nintendo or watch TV. And the kids would not pay much attention at night to their dad. And the reason why these kids were not listening to them and having problems with their wives is because they are not giving them any time for them to work on their relationship with each other. They are working too much and chasing that almighty dollar around and sacrificing their families in the process.

"Money never made a man happy yet, nor will it. There is nothing in its nature to produce happiness. The more a man has, the more he wants. Instead of its filling a vacuum, it makes one. If it satisfies one want, it doubles and trebles that want another way. That was a true proverb of the wise man, rely upon it: 'Better is little with the fear of the Lord,

than great treasure, and trouble therewith,'"[ii] Benjamin
Franklin said this. Or how about George Horace Lorimer,
"It's good to have money and the things that money can buy,
but it's good, too, to check up once in a while and make sure
that you haven't lost the things that money can't buy."[iii] And
it is those relationships that they are losing. But if you think
about it, what is easier. Making money or working on a relationship. Money you can physically see and everyone
knows what he or she is supposed to do to earn it. However
in a relationship it is an ongoing thing. You have some good
days and some bad. It is an intangible, it is hard to measure
your progress.

Now different types of jobs obviously have different
types of pay scales and different forms of pay. For instance
when I was in the trades the salesmen for the company
were paid on commission. They had incentive to go out and
find as much business as they wanted, and the more business the more money. They were only paid when they were
able to find work. And when I came out of college I was
offered a commission-based job, selling stocks, bonds, and
mutual funds. Which I hear was very hard, and I decided
that was not the route I was going to take. But these companies in this area have very high turn over rate, especially in
the first two years. I think that it is kind of difficult to live
and not know how much money you are going to have at
the end of the month to pay your bills. But there are some
people that love this kind of work. They love to interact
with customers and the thrill of closing a deal. Sometimes
there are different lunches and golf outings that play a role
in all of this. Trying to encourage the prospective customer
to go through with it. And obviously some customers are
easier than others.

I remember shopping for a new family car with my dad.
We went to several dealerships and stayed there for a few
hours. My dad would just talk to the salesman and find out

everything he could about the different makes and models. And then he would have to come home and check things on the Internet to make sure what he was being told by the sales person was correct. So then he narrowed down his choices a little bit and then he went back for round two. And then finally he decided on a car, but then he had to decide about the financing aspect. Which was not nearly as bad as choosing the make and the model. But needless to say he spends a lot of his evenings going around to different car dealerships. And on top of that sales person spend a lot of time investing in my dad, hoping that he would end up and buy a car from them. But that is their job as being a car salesman is to try to persuade people to buy cars from them and that dealership. And a big part of that is spending time with the customer to figure out what kind of car he is interested in and the price ranges it. And what motivates those car sales people is the commission they will receive from the sale of the car.

On top of commission, people are paid salary. These people know how much they are going to make within a certain amount of time. Salaried employees usually have a certain amount of work that has to be done or a certain amount of time that they need to spend in the office to receive that pay. For instance working for the bank, I was paid a salary. I knew that I was expected to be at work Monday through Friday, from 8:30 to 5. These types of employees don't really have a whole lot of incentives to go out and bring in new business, of course it doesn't look bad. But it is not a big part of their job. I tend to think that these people may tend to be a little more conservative.

Another sources of income that some companies give out are bonuses. Which both commission and salary people can get bonuses. Whether it is because you exceeded your sales goal or the company did really well and they decided that they are going to share the profits with the employees.

And bonuses try to make the employees work together to maximize the company's profits.

So in this world there are all kinds of ways people make a living and are compensated for it. Looking at the kingdom of Heaven I think is a little different. I almost look at it, that Christians are rewarded by God in a combination of all three ways: commission, salary, and bonus.

We are told to "Remember this: Whoever sows sparingly will also reap sparingly, and whoever sows generously will also reap generously" (2 Corinthians 9:6). So if we do a lot of investing in other people for the work of God's kingdom. I really believe that we will in a sense be rewarded by encouragement from people coming to know Christ. Just to hear that so and so are going to try to work out their marriage instead of just getting a divorce. And the reason why they are going to work on their marriage is because you were willing to listen to him or her. Or whatever the situation maybe. I think that I would be encouraged because God used me to have some influence in their decision.

Of course there are going to be some people that are going to receive the word of God better than others. Jesus talks about the parable of the Sower in Matthew. "Then he told them many things in parables, saying, "A farmer went out to sow his seed. As he was scattering the seed, some fell along the path, and the birds came and ate it up. Some fell on rocky places, where it did not have much soil. It sprang up quickly, because the soil was shallow. But when then sun came up, the plants were scorched, and they withered because they had no root. Other seed fell among thorns, which grew up and choked the plants. Still other seed fell on good soil, where it produced a crop a hundred, sixty or thirty times what was sown. He who has ears let him hear." "Listen then to what the parable of the sower means: When anyone hears the message about the kingdom and does not understand it, the evil one comes and snatches away what was sown in his heart. This is the seed sown along the path. The one who received the seed that fell on the rocky places is the man who hears the word and at once receives it with joy. But since he has no root, he lasts only a short time. When trouble or persecution comes because of the word, he quickly falls away. The one who received the seed that fell among the thorns is the man who hears the word, but the worries of this life and the deceitfulness of wealth choke it, making it unfruitful. But the one who received the seed that fell on good soil is the man who hears the word and understands it. He produces a crop, yielding a hundred, sixty or thirty times what was sown" (Matthew 13:3-9 and 18-23). And in those situations it might be very discouraging. Like trying to be one of these salesmen that my dad had dealt with. Because we invest our valuable time in people, that hopefully one day they might come to know Christ. However they decided not to at this point in time. Hopefully we are going to see it worthwhile to invest time into someone, and it gets discouraging when nothing happens. Or at least when we think nothing is happening.

"Even now the reaper draws his wages, even now he harvests the crop for eternal life, so that the sower and the reaper may be glad together. Thus the saying 'One sows and another reaps' is true. I sent you to reap what you have not worked for. Others have done the hard work, and you have reaped the benefits of their labor" (John 4:36-38). But we have to take that chance and invest that time in people, unfortunately we might not be the one to "close the deal" on that person, but we just need to pray that God places someone else in their lives to reach that person. "He told them, 'the harvest is plentiful, but the workers are few. Ask the Lord of the harvest, therefore, to send out workers into the harvest field'" (Luke 10:2). The good thing about Christianity is that it should be a team effort. We should not worry if we "close the deal" or if someone else does, it is all for the glory of God.

And God does not require us to close so many deals in order to get into Heaven. And that is where our salary part comes in. And this is where our bonuses come in we are working together for one cause. And reaping the rewards together.

Like we said earlier a salary person knows what they are going to receive on their paycheck. We as Christians are no different. We know "that if you confess with your mouth, 'Jesus is Lord,' and believe in your heart that God raised him from the dead, you will be saved. For it is with your heart that you believe and are justified, and it is with your mouth that you confess and are saved" (Romans 10:9-10). And this is how we know that we are one of God's children, a Christian. We also know that "our citizenship is in heaven. And we eagerly await a Savior from there, the Lord Jesus Christ" (Philippians 3:20). So according to these scriptures all we have to do is just live our lives for Christ. Which often times means that we have to change, which is not an over night thing, and each person has different things they have to change. I know before giving my life to Christ I was always very negative and hard on people. My thought life is still a constant struggle. But I am working on these areas of my life to reflect how Jesus would be. I am working on these areas because I love Jesus and want to live my life according to how He wants me too. And that is why this kind of relates to our salary. We know that we are suppose to change and suppose to pray and suppose to share our faith. And we know what we will receive in the end because of our faith and Grace of Jesus Christ.

So if we as Christians are able to go to Heaven without bringing anyone else to Christ or doing anything else: feeding the homeless, giving to charities, visiting people in the hospital. After all our salary of a Christian is Heaven, we know that we are guaranteed that. Why do Christians bother to do different things? "In the same way, faith by itself, if it is not accompanied by action, is dead" (James 2:17).

Rich Mullins even wrote a song about it, he titled it Screen Door. And a couple of the lines read, "Faith without works, Is like a song you can't sing, it's about as useless as, a screen door on a submarine."[iv] Now you really don't have to think about that, no submarine is going to have a screen door on it. That would allow all the water to come. God's gift of grace is amazing and we should be really excited to share it with others whether that be by words or actions. "I pray that you may be active in sharing your faith, so that you will have a full understanding of every good thing we have in Christ" (Philemon 1:6).

So living as a Christian is not always easy. We come in contact with a lot of people that are both encouraging and discouraging to our faith. And some of those encouraging times are almost going to be like bonuses, little rewards, from what we are doing here on earth for Christ. But we will also have times in our lives that we are going to be challenged to our faith but we must remember that one day we are going to receive our reward, and our savior will take us home. "Let us not become weary in doing good, for at the proper time we will reap a harvest if we do not give up" (Galatians 6:9). And it is so easy to give up when things get tough, but sometimes we have to stand our ground. And it is when we stand our ground and the sky clears, the clouds roll over. It is then that we get the satisfaction of victory for Christ. "Blessed is the man who perseveres under trial, because when he has stood the test, he will receive the crown of life that God has promised to those who love him" (James 1:12). "The way to Heaven is ascending; we must be content to travel up hill, though it be hard and tiresome, and contrary to the natural bias of our flesh,[v]" Jonathan Edwards: The Christian Pilgrim. "This is a trustworthy saying. And I want you to stress these things, so that those who have trusted in God may be careful to devote themselves to doing what is good. These things are excellent and profitable for everyone" (Titus 3:8). Profitable, we recognize that word, don't we. So let us remember that we might not get paid in dollars but we will be rewarded. And it will be better than any paycheck anyone can ever get. Let us remember it will last all of Eternity. And we will be dancing on golden streets; money is going to have no value. So lets not get caught up in chasing the almighty dollar, because in reality it is not that almighty.

The CEO

"Instead, I have called you friends, for everything that I learned from my Father I have made know to you".

John 15:15

For many people, especially those who work in the fortune 500 companies may never meet the CEO or the Board of Directors. And if they do they may not have wanted too. Also if the CEO would meet you they would probably not remember your name. Of course it all depends on where you are at in the company and how big the company is. Working at a smaller organization and the position that I was given I did meet most of the directors along with the upper management.

I had the privilege of having lunch with the president of the bank. Each month the president of the bank would take out the employees who had a birthday in that month. Given we were only a company of a couple/three hundred employees. And I thought this was a great idea, and really admire him for doing this. But there we sat at the table; there was about a dozen of us. Of course some were more talkative than others. For some it was first time meeting the president, which in turn they were pretty quiet. But I was one of the first ones to get to the restaurant. And I was sitting talking with the ones already there and as people walked by us he was not sure if they were employees or just other people using the restaurant. I enjoyed the lunch and I was able to meet some people that I would have never met otherwise.

I can recall another instance when I was sitting at one of the locations and the manager was paged. So she looked at her pager, and didn't recognize the pager number and had to look it up. And sure enough it was the CEO paging her. She didn't know him to well, so she asked a number of people frantically why he was pager her. And one of the bankers made a comment that it is not a good thing when you are page by him, that hopefully he paged the wrong person. Well she called him back and got his voice mail, never really sure what came of it.

Again when I was at the flooring company, the owner would come out, again a small business. And would get on the installers case about moving to slow, and that they need to speed things up, that he was losing money on this job. Well the installers didn't care much for that kind of pep talk. They would put up with him while he was on the job site, but then as soon as he would leave they would curse his name, and usually take a little break. So for some people the President's of our company's are people we don't relate to. It seems like the only time we talk to them is when something goes wrong. And they don't remember the good things we have done.

We as Christians have a boss also. We have to answer to Jesus, He's our CEO. We are told in Acts: "As surely as I live, says the Lord, 'every knee will bow before me; every tongue will confess to God.' So then, each of us will give an account of himself to God" (Romans 14:11-12). And it is better to do that ahead of time than at the time when Jesus comes back. Also told Jesus will judge us. He will judge ou hearts and actions. Which we are kind of used to, having people watching us and calling us on our faults, just like many of our bosses. But we should not worry because "For we do not have a high priest who is unable to sympathize with our weaknesses, but we have one who has been tempted in every way, just as we are – yet without sin. Let us then approach the throne of grace with confidence, so that we may receive mercy and find grace to help us in our time of need" (Hebrews 4:15-16). That is kind of a relief. It is almost like someone who has worked their way up the corporate ladder and understands all the functions and stress of the different jobs, along with life in general. It is when you hear people working up the corporate ladder. Saying that they will not forget where they came from. Well Christ truly didn't forget what He had to go through.

We also know and have to constantly remind ourselves that we are "for God's workmanship, created in Christ Jesus to do good works, which God prepared in advance for us to do" (Ephesians 2:10). God know us and desires to have a relationship with us. Usually in business you are someone's best friend only when you can help him or her out some how, some way. And once you help them out you are left in the dust. Not with God. "And even the very hairs of your head are all numbered. So don't be afraid; you're worth more than many sparrows" (Matthew 10:30-31). He wants us to come to him in times of need. He wants us to let our "guard down" when we come to Him. We don't have to put on an act for Him, we are just fooling ourselves.

God is not worried about production, or how many people you bring to Christ each year. There is no quota. Some people have a gift of evangelism. So those people may lead a lot of people to Christ. That is awesome first of all that people are coming to know Christ. I should be happy for both the person that decided to live their life for Christ and the person that brought them to the truth. But at the same time that doesn't mean that we get off easy. You will be able to reach other types of people and personalities than I or someone else would be able to and vice versa.

But you may enjoy serving others or encouraging others. We need to use those gifts, but there is no quota. God wants us to remain focused on Jesus and as long as that happens God will be with us and provide opportunities for us. "Delight yourself in the Lord and he will give you the desires of your heart" (Psalm 37:4). Jesus is there to help us through anything and everything we go through in life. He wants to help us; He is not there shaking his finger at us. "I have told you these things, so that in me you may have peace. In this world you will have trouble. But take heart! I have overcome the world" (John 16:33).

Also when we have a problem in the business world, we have a chain of command. You see it in the army all of the time. You have someone that you report to and then that person has someone he/she reports to and so on. Now it causes some problems when an employee has a problem with something or someone and they go to the person above their manager. Often times the manager doesn't like that because your manager usually gets in trouble for not taking care of the problem. So the manger hears about it from their manager so the manager then usually has some sort of talk with the employee. Now most employees are not too happy about this especially if they don't have that good of manager. Sometimes your manager is playing favorites, or has a pride issue. And nothing ever changes, which then frustrates the employee even more.

Once again with Christianity it is different. We have a direct line with God, our maker, and ruler over the universe. We can use that line anytime that we want to. In fact we are told that we should always be using it, "Pray continually" (1 Thessalonians 5:17). Whether it be a praise or a request or just to talk. Once again he wants to have a relationship with us, more than just hello how's your day going? He wants to know everything about us, our hurts, our dreams, fears; He does listen to us and is interested in us. Henry Ward Beecher says this about prayer: "Prayer covers the whole of a man's life. There is no thought, feeling, yearning, or desire, however low, trifling, or vulgar we may deem it, which, if it affects our real interest or happiness, we may not lay before God and be sure of sympathy. His nature is such that our often coming does not tire Him. The whole burden of the whole life of every man may be rolled on to God and not weary him, though it has wearied the man."[vi] And let us not get distracted by the word prayer. It is simply a crying out and talking to God. "The best style of prayer is that which cannot be call anything but a cry," Charles Spurgeon.

So let us not stereotype God like we do to other CEOs. Let's use Him as a resource, his knowledge is our power, tap into it. Remember God does treat us really good; he takes good care of us. "He does not treat us as our sins deserve or repay us according to our iniquities" (Psalm 103:10). It would be kind of scary if we were treated according to our sins. So let's remember: "'God has said, 'Never will I leave you; never will I forsake you'" (Hebrews 13:5).

Our Fellow Employees

"For where two or three come together in my name, there am I with them".

Matthew 18:20

When you have people that work together as a team, things seem to go a lot smoother. Your employee retention rate seems to be higher and you are able to be more efficient. In my Management trainee program I rotated around to a number of different branches and departments. I was able to meet and work with a lot of different people. Some people I really enjoyed working with and some locations I was happy when my time was up. The best way to learn is just to get your hands dirty and do it. And that is what I did; when I was a relationship banker I was opening accounts. Doing what a relation banker does. Well at first I didn't really know what I was doing, so I had a lot of question. And of course nothing was cut and dry, you would have a customer that would want to come in and open a CD, but not a regular CD an IRA or a trust account. Well I was at a branch that didn't work so well as a team, they were kind of worried about their loan numbers and doing there own thing. Trying to make sure that they were looking good. Well I can tell you I didn't ask as many questions because I didn't feel people wanted to help as much. I felt more like a hindrance to them. So I would try to muscle through it, I even called different employees at different branches for help. Also this took more time. Which meant that people had to wait a little longer.

Now the point that I am making is we need to be willing to help fellow believers out in times of need. We need to be unified. We need to use our spiritual gifts together as one body. That is how God calls us to be. We should not get caught up in the different denominations, race, or age. We need to see through all of those things. There is power when we meet, "for where two or three come together in my name, there am I with them" (Matthew 18:20). We also need to check up on each other. And see how we can help each other out. "Therefore confess your sins to each other and pray for each other so that you may be healed. The prayer of a righteous man is powerful and effective" (James 5:16). Let us not forget what the Bible says about confessing our sins, "If we confess our sins, he is faithful and just and will forgive us our sins and purify us from all unrighteousness" (1 John 1:9).

We sometimes to have to make sacrifices when we are working together or going to help someone else out. But I think that Christ would help others out. I am not saying that we are to do all of the work for others. But if they need help getting started or if they are experiencing computer problems, I am sure that you know how frustrating that can be. Or maybe they have not been feeling to well the last couple of days. Or maybe we have a little more experience in a certain area and we notice that they are kind of struggling. Yes it may be an inconvenience for us. But those little things can make a big difference in those people's lives. Wouldn't we appreciate it done for us also? Plus we never know how God is going to use you.

I believe that we can use the situation in our lives to help others out. Maybe a close friend just past away, well I had a close friend past away last year. So I should try to comfort them, because I know how it feels because I just went through it last year. Maybe I had the same questions about Christianity. And I can share what helped me answer those questions. Or an abortion, divorce, or drug abuse. We could use those bad situations that we went through to help others to try to avoid some of the same pain that we went through. But we have to be willing to open ourselves up to those people. That is where it gets risky for us. I really do believe that God will honor that. I also think that it's a shame if we go through that horrible situation and then we hide them. "Therefore, if anyone is in Christ, he is anew creation; the old has gone, the new has come" (2 Corinthians 5:17). I know people are worried how people are going to accept them after sharing about their past, and if those same people that we share with if they are going judge us about our past. We have to remember that it is not by those people that we are saved. It's Jesus and only Jesus that has the final say.

We need to stop trying to out do each other. It is all for God's glory, that's all that matters. We're one body, we are a team. You don't see professional football teams beating up on each other and bringing each other down. It's so foolish.

Again with the position I had at the bank, I learned just about every aspect of every position at the bank. When there was a problem in one department that needed help from another department. I was able to know whom to call. And since I knew of the exact person to contact to fix the problem I was able to eliminate more downtime by calling so and so and then them telling me to call someone else, or even offending them by asking them to do something that was not their job. I could also tell you that the higher up in management I got in the bank the less of those people knew who actually did the work. Of course they knew the managers of the departments, for when they would call in their favors. But they had no idea exactly the process that they had to go through and the people that were doing the work. Sometimes upper management would separate themselves; they looked down on the other employees. I also believed that it really helps putting a name with a face, it made it a little more personal.

To be an effective Church I believe that we have to do the same thing. We need to know who has what gifts. We need to use those gifts for one common purpose, glorifying God. And we need to be able to work together, as one body. This involved conversations and spending time with one another, within the Church. I encourage all of us to go out to dinner with each other, or have people over. We all have to eat. So why not slow down a little and go out with some people from church or invite someone over for a meal. But ask the hard, spiritual questions. Ask what kind of spiritual gifts they have, or how they came to know Christ. Ask what you can pray for. This is how we will be able to become more of a community. I know it's hard, I don't like it always. I am a very shallow person, and I like my privacy. But we need to take that step of faith and get out of our comfort zone, that's when God uses us. That's when He really blesses us. I truly believe that if this happens we will be able to reach out to more people more effectively than we are doing now. Because we are working together not against each other.

When I was going through my training I was able to meet a lot of people. I was in one particular department; it was a back office setting. So the language and attitudes of people were a little more relaxed. Opinions were shared a little more openly. One of the guys down there would completely rip on his boss. He would just go on and on about how bad of a manger he was and how he didn't agree with how he did things. It was awful. There was such a tension there between the two. And guess what whenever one needed something from another, it didn't happen right away.

Another gentleman that kind of has took me under his wing. He had a couple of boys like me and just watching out for them. He had also been in the business for a while and was just looking out for me; he had some advice to offer me. But you know what he told me was to find out who had power and align myself with those people. Do anything that I can to make myself known to them and be recognized by them. And that if I would do that, those people would protect me. So basically if I was working on something and someone with power within the company came to me with a problem or a project I should take care of them first, not just the average Joe.

This kind of goes against what God says. He tells us that we should not show favoritism. "My brothers, as believers in our glorious Lord Jesus Christ, don't show favoritism. Suppose a man comes into your meeting wearing a gold ring and fine clothes, and a poor man in shabby clothes also comes in. If you show special attention to the man wearing fine clothes and say, 'here is a good seat for you,' but say to the poor man, 'you stand there' or 'sit on the floor by me feet,' have you not discriminated among yourselves and become judges with evil thoughts? Listen, my dear brothers: has not God chosen those who are poor in the eyes of the world to be rich in faith and to inherit the kingdom he promised those who love him? But you have insulted the poor. Is it not he rich who are exploiting you? Are they not the ones who are dragging you into court? Are they not the ones who are slandering the noble name of him to who you belong" (James 2:1-7)?

In fact God wants the average Joe. He wants the everyday people, not the power hungry and prideful people. Again in the Bible it talks about the disciples and how they were just average, uneducated people. But they knew Christ and were living their lives for Christ. And that's what we have to do. All throughout the Proverbs God warns the Proud. Those people that are in power now in corporate America, if they don't know Jesus as their own personal Lord and Savior they are going to be judged just like you and I. They won't have any advantages or different standards than you and I. The grave is the ultimate equalizer. "As for those who seemed to be important – whatever they were makes no difference to me; God does not judge by external appearance – those men added nothing to my message" (Galatians 2:6). It is Jesus that has the "Power" we need to have a relationship with him. "I am the way and the truth and the life. No one comes to the Father except through me" (John 14:6). So I guess my co-worker was right, we need to align ourselves with power, which is Jesus. And if we do that we will be okay.

Working Together

"Just as each of us has one body with many members, and these members do not all have the same function, so in Christ we who are many form one body, and each member belongs to all the others".

Romans 12:4

At the bank we have various departments. I am sure that a few different departments come to mind. Such as the tellers and loan officers. However there are plenty more that people are not real familiar with. And of course they all do different things. Some departments are on the 'front line' where they have to deal with customers all day long. Then other departments we called 'back office,' they never see any customers. Different people like the different areas better to work in than the other. It just kind of depends on their character and personality. In fact the 'back office' customers are the 'front line' employees. And believe me both sides have their differences. Of course the 'front line' people wanted to make the customer happy, so they would not have to hear the customers complain. But the back office people also want to make sure everything is done properly so when the bank was audited by the OCC they meet all the requirements. So actually it is a good checks and balance system. So needless to say not everyone gets along. A big reason for all of the confusion was the 'front line' people don't know what the 'back office' people do and vs. versa. And actually that was part of my job when I was first hired. Was to go through the whole bank to understand how everything works together. And let me tell you I got to hear all of the stories and a few choice words about a couple of people and departments. But it worked. Now I have respect for what everyone does at the bank. And now I know if I ever have a problem who to contact without offending anyone in the process. Also I know who actually works and who is dependable.

But do you know what is interesting. Especially since we are an employee owned bank. Is that we were working for a common purpose. And that was working to increase the bottom line of the bank's income statement. We all benefited from that, being a employee owned bank. So why do we bump our heads so much?

I kind of think that it is the same with Christianity. We have one purpose and that is to share Jesus Christ with others along with living our lives for Him. We can look at the great commission that Jesus left us with: "Therefore go and make disciples of all nations, baptizing them in the name of the Father and of the Son and of the Holy Spirit, and teaching them to obey everything I have commanded you. And surely I am with you always, to the very end of the age" (Matthew 28:19-20). And throughout the Bible we read and learn that we are not expected to do this alone. We are allowed to work together. "Just as each of us has one body with many members, and these members do not all have the same function, so in Christ we who are many form one body, and each member belongs to all the others"

(Romans 12:4). And I believe that God gave us different gifts for a reason. "It was he who gave some to be apostles, some to be prophets, some to be evangelists, and some to be pastors and teachers, to prepare God's people for works of service, so that the body of Christ may be built up until we all reach unity in the faith and in knowledge of the Son of God and become mature, attaining to the whole measure of the fullness of Christ" (Ephesians 4:11-13). Different people reach different people. And different gifts are used in different ways in the Church. Since we have different gifts we have to allow each other to use them accordingly. "We have different gifts, according to the grace given us. If a man's gift is prophesying, let him use it in proportion to his faith. If it is serving, let him serve; if it is teaching, let him teach; if it is encouraging, let him encourage; if it is contributing to the needs of others, let him give generously; if it is leadership, let him govern diligently; if it is showing mercy, let him do it cheerfully" (Romans 12:6-8). So those people are going to be very visible to everyone. People are going to know what they are doing and how they are impacting people and the church. Just like the 'front line' people at the bank, which is similar to the tellers and loan officers. You know what a teller is doing when you give them a check to cash or making a deposit. However there are some people that have the gift of service. Now these people I would classify as 'back room' people. Half the time we don't know who is doing the sound system, or who is setting up chairs, or organizing events. But you know with out those 'back room' people that front line people won't be as effective. And with out the 'front line' people the back room people won't have any reason to do what they do. So we need each other.

So what are spiritual gifts? Here are some of the different Spiritual gifts: apostles, prophets, teachers, miracles, healing, administrations, tongues, faith, helps, evangelists, and encouragement are some of the gifts mentioned throughout the Bible. According to Michael Griffiths, "gifts are not personal attributes or acquisitions, but rather outpourings of God's grace."[vii] These gifts are Gods way of equipping each of us to complete the work that God has planned for us. It is one way that God makes us unique in His eyes. "Each one should use whatever gift he has received to serve others, faithfully administering God's grace in it various forms" (1 Peter 4:10). We all have different gifts; we all play a different position in the church. So let us keep our focus on the warning that Paul gives us, "Do not neglect your gift, which was given you through a prophetic message when the body of elders laid their hands on you" (1Timothy 4:14). I think that it is very easy to get in the habit of thinking that we can't make a difference and that we aren't a vital part of the body of Christ. But that is Satan lying to us. So let us use our gifts so that they don't go to waste. "So it is with you. Since you are eager to have spiritual gifts, try to excel in the gifts that build up the church" (1 Corinthians 14:12).

If we think that we don't have any gifts or that God can't use us. Again that is Satan lying to us. "Each one should use whatever gift he has received" (1 Peter 4:10). It doesn't say use the gifts if you receive them, but that we have received them and we need to use them. It is the Holy Spirit that gives us these gifts. "All these are the work of one and the same Spirit, and he gives them to each one, just as he determines" (1 Corinthians 12:11). So not only does the Holy Spirit give us our gifts, but he gives us the gifts for a specific reason. And if we are unsure about our gifts there are multiple ways that we can go about finding them out. First we can also talk to another Christian and ask them what gifts they feel that we have. Second there are different questionnaires that you can always fill out, which you can find at the local Christian bookstore. Third we can also pray about our gifts that we come to recognize what are gifts are and how to use them.

We are called to be one body in Christ. "The body is a unit, though it is made up of many parts; and though all its parts are many, they form one body. So it is with Christ. For we were all baptized by one Spirit into one body - whether Jews or Greeks, slave or free – and we were all given the one Spirit to drink. Now the body is not made up of one part but of many. If the foot should say, 'because I am not a hand, I do not belong to the body,' it would not for that reason cease to be part of the body. And if the ear should say, 'because I am not an eye, I do not belong to the body,' it would not for that reason cease to be part of the body. If the whole body were an eye, where would the sense of hearing be? If the whole body were an ear, where would the sense of smell be? But in fact God has arranged the parts in the body, every one of them, just as he wanted them to be. If they were all one part, where would the body be? As it is, there are many parts, but one body. The eye cannot say to the hand, ' I don't need you!' And the head cannot say to the feet, 'I don't need you!' On the contrary, those parts of the body that seem to be weaker are indispensable, and the parts that we think are less honorable we treat with special honor. And the parts that are unpresentable are treated with special modesty, while our presentable parts need no special treatment. But God has combined the members of the body and has given greater honor to the parts that lack it, so that there should be no division in the body, but that its parts should have equal concern for each other. If one part suffers, every part suffers with it; if one part is honored, every part rejoices with it" (1 Corinthians 12:12-26). So let's act like it. Let's stop arguing and complaining with each other. Let's realize what our parts are in the body and make the most of it. Obviously God gave us those gifts for a reason. Can you image what kind of impact we would have on our communities if we work together?

We have to appreciate each other but we should be careful about always patting our selves on the back. God warns us about trying to work too much on our own and he cautions us about taking all of the praise and credit. "For by the grace given me I say to everyone of you: Do not think of yourself more highly that you ought, but rather think of yourself with sober judgment, in accordance with the measure of faith God has given you" (Romans 12:3). "Let another praise you, and not your own mouth; someone else, and not your own lips" (Proverbs 27:2). We need to remember, "For everyone who exalts himself will be humbled, and he who humbles himself will be exalted (Luke 18:14)." We are also reminded and asked the question: "Am I now trying to win the approval of men, or of God? Or am I trying to please men? If I were still trying to please men, I would not be a servant of Christ" (Galatians 1:10). If we are trying to out do one another and gain praise and acceptance from each other we are wasting our time. God doesn't want that. And besides God knows our hearts, he knows what we do when no one else is looking. "But when you pray, go into your room, close the door and pray to your Father, who is unseen. Then your Father, who sees what is done in secret, will reward you" (Matthew 6:6). Jesus is the only one that is going to Judge us, "There is only one Lawgiver and Judge, the one who is able to save and destroy. But you – who are you to judge your neighbor" (James 4:12)? So lets not try to go out of our way to always try to gain praise from other people.

"Surely you remember, brothers, our toil and hardship; we worked night and day in order not to be a burden to anyone while we preached the gospel of God to you" (1 Thessalonians 2:9). We have to remember also that working together to reach others is not always easy. It requires a lot of sacrifice on our parts. Of course everyone being busy some will have to rearrange their schedules to do their part. What Paul was writing about in 1 Thessalonians, is very true. It is not always going to be easy, there are going to be some hardships. Working for God is not a cut and dry, 9 to 5 job. Sometimes it maybe getting up early to go out to breakfast with someone or getting a phone call at 2 am. We need to make ourselves available to others in order to be used by God. "On the contrary, we speak as men approved by God to be entrusted with the gospel. We are not trying to please men but God, who test our hearts. You know we never used flattery, nor did we put on a mask to cover up greed – God is our witness. We were not looking for praise from men, not from you or anyone else" (1 Thessalonians 2:4-6). That brings up another good point. We should not be doing what we are doing for personal praise. We need to keep our focus on Christ and make the appropriate sacrifices. We will be rewarded at a later time.

Training

"But as for you, continue in what you have learned and have become convinced of, because you know those from whom you learned it, and how from infancy you have known the holy Scriptures, which are able to make you wise for salvation through faith in Christ Jesus".
2 Timothy 3:14-15

In business you need to know what you are doing. Companies are trying to be as efficient as they can so they can maximize their profits. Companies spend millions of dollars on training programs and seminars each year. Some of these different seminars and training programs are for team building among departments, new laws that have been passed, new products that are on the market, leadership, etc. If you look at Public Accounting Firms their employees have to be up to date with all the new tax law changes. It's required that CPA's have so many hours each year of classroom to keep their job, to keep their title.

Companies when they first hire people have some sort of training for their new employees or some sort of shadow program. Even after they get out of college. Companies must believe that its worth it or otherwise they would not waste time and money doing it. The better-trained people will perform better in there jobs.

When I first got out of college I was hired as a Management Trainee. I was going to be spending time in all the different departments of the bank. I spent time as a teller, to item processing, to auditing, to trust, to lending, I had a chance to do it all. And at the end of the year of training I was not necessarily going to be a manger. I could end up almost anywhere. But this company was making an investment in me. They were training me. They were trying to develop me right out of college, which I didn't have any bad habits yet, concerning the work place. And they were hoping that by having me do all of this, that I would have a general understanding about banking and knew how everything worked. So that if something went wrong in the future I would know who and how it effects, along with who to contact and possibly how to fix it. It was obvious what the bank was doing. The bank was training me.

Many people make their living traveling around the country giving motivational speeches, seminars and training sessions. We would have them come in at school. They were especially big in high school right before prom, against drinking and driving. But we also see financial seminars, such as: retirement planning, mutual funds, 401K plans, and investment properties. People have figured out how you should be saving and they want to tell you but also charge you. People are standing at the doors just to hear these "financial wizards" speak. Or companies have huge conferences to introduce new products to its sales force, along with motivating them to sell their products and services.

I am learning that in the business world you are never through with learning. There is something new always coming out whether it is new tax laws, new computer software or new products, you need to stay up with the times otherwise you and your company will get passed by.

Christianity is the same way. It is continually a learning process. I almost think that the more you try to know Christ; you realize how little you know about him. Our key training manual is our Bible. It is God's word. It is 100% truth. The Bible tells us how we should live how we should handle the situations that we come into contact with. The Bible gives us words of encouragement in times of need. We are told that the Bible is "For the word of God is living and active. Sharper than any double edged sword, it penetrates even to dividing soul and spirit, joints and marrow; it judges the thoughts and attitudes of the heart" (Hebrews 4:12). And since the Bible is so powerful, we need to be in the Bible daily. We need to know it inside and out. I know that it is a lot of stuff and not always exciting. Some of it is pretty crazy like Pharaoh's plagues, we find them in Exodus 7:14 to 8:15. But how funny is the plague of frogs, where there were frogs everywhere, even in the food. But there are times that we can encourage a fellow brother or sister in Christ by quoting a scripture to them. There have been plenty of times where I have gotten down on life and myself because things were not going how I had planned or wanted. But people have encouraged me through different verses such as: "and we know that in all things God works for the good of those who love him, who have been called according to his purpose" (Romans 8:28). It can be something extremely simple but I find comfort and oftentimes I need to be reminded of God's word. Or a time that you might be in your office and a coworker has a 'religious' question for you but you don't have time to look it up. They might ask do you really believe that Jesus is the only God? "Jesus answered, 'I am the way and the truth and the life. No one comes to the Father except through me" (John 14:6). That is going to show a lot of power if you could just quote a verse of the top of your head. I think that shows that you really are passionate about what you believe. Besides if you are a salesman and someone asks you a question. Won't you look bad if you have to go into your sales manual to find the answer? If you are a good sales person you know your product inside and out. Not that we are necessarily selling Christ but being a Christian is a way of life and we should know everything that we can about our faith.

And in times of temptation I have found that if you can quote scripture, and it really helps you over come the temptation. There are examples how to get out of that possible sinful temptation. We look at Joseph, he just plainly ran away. "One day he went into the house to attend to his duties, and none of the household servants was inside. She caught him by his cloak and said, 'Come to bed with me!' But he left his cloak in her hand and ran out of the house" (Genesis 39:11-12). Sometimes I think that we try to make it to complicated. Also quoting scripture can give us the encouragement and the strength to just say no. Your focus is usually changed and Satan can't stand that. Because Jesus does say, "no temptation has seized you except what is common to man. And God is faithful; he will not let you be tempted beyond what you can bear. But when you are tempted, he will also provide a way out so that you can stand up under it" (1 Corinthians 10:13). We can look at Jesus when He was in the desert, how Jesus responded to the tempting of the devil in this manner. "It is also written: 'do not put the Lord your God to the test" (Matthew 4:7). Do you know where you can find that? You can find that in Deuteronomy 6:16, that's right Jesus quoted Scripture to resist the devil. If it worked for him why won't it work for us? And I really think that is a easy way out of temptation. I think that we recognize that we are in need of God and it shifts our focus onto Christ and not ourselves. If you look at the story about Joseph when Potiphar's wife tried to seduce him. He simply ran, he even ran naked, he didn't care he just wanted to get out of there before something happened. I really think that a lot of times we underestimate the power there is in reading the Bible.

Another training ground for Christians is the Church. Church has many ways that we are trained for Christ. The Sermons alone are a way that people grow in Christ and learn more about Christ. I do encourage you to go to your Bible and look up what the sermon is about to make sure that it is Biblical. Along with this book you are reading here. Just confirm it to God's word, if nothing else it just reinforces it and helps us to become more familiar with God's word. The worship even during the Church service helps us to see God in a different light. Helps us to realize how great he really is to us.

Also within most Churches they have small groups of people that get together and discuss a number of different topics. Small groups have ranged from spiritual gifts, relationships, money, etc. I have read through plenty of books with people within the Church. We use each chapter as conversation starters and then go from there. Which some books are better than others. Some books are more open ended which makes for better conversation. Some books now even have discussion questions in the back of the book to help start discussion in the group. I have also been a part of groups that strictly just read through the Bible and then discuss the section they read through. In addition to those groups the Church that I belong to has a new members class. Which is for people that have recently given their lives to Christ and want to join our Church. It helps them to have a basic understanding what it means to live their lives for Christ.

We also have seminars and speakers that God uses to encourage us. I had the opportunity to go to a seminar on Credit Analysis, which was only a day and half, was going to cost a little less than a thousand dollars. Now that is a lot of money. And that doesn't include any traveling. So how come we are willing to spend all this money on business seminars but when it comes to different Christian seminars it is too much. Isn't our soul so much more important than our wallets and egos? But just like business seminars Christian seminars are usually on specific topics or for specific groups. Such as Promise Keepers. They are directed towards men and usually fill stadiums full of men and have speakers from all across the nation speak to them. I realize conferences don't save us, but they sure can help inspire us and light that fire again for Christ.

Just like business, it is a never-ending process of learning. However our learning and understanding will last forever. And we say that we just are too busy to go to Church, to be in a small group to go to that conference. Don't we owe it to God to spend time in the word and prayer and with others since we do it all the time in the business world? Remember that "Do not deceive yourselves. If any one of you thinks he is wise by the standards of this age, he should become a 'fool' so that he may become wise. For the wisdom of this world is foolish in God's sight" (1 Corinthians 3:18-19).

I really think that these few verses really hit it on the head. "But as for you, continue in what you have learned and have become convinced of, because you know those from whom you learned it, and how from infancy you have known the holy Scriptures which are able to make you wise for salvation through faith in Christ Jesus. All Scripture is God-Breathed and is useful for teaching, rebuking, correcting and training in righteousness, so that the man of God may be thoroughly equipped for every good work" (2 Timothy 3:14-17). There is nothing more to say.

Customer Service

"If someone forces you to go one mile, go with him two miles".

Matthew 5:41

The banking industry is a unique industry. It is highly regulated and extremely competitive. The big difference between banks is the customer service. And that was drilled into my head. Make sure you introduce yourself, ask if there is anything else you could do for the customer. There was a lot of follow up that was required just to make sure that the customer was happy and remembered you and most importantly the bank. And if they weren't happy we were supposed to go out of our way to make them happy, of course within reason.

Just to get on my soapbox for a second. Also in order to understand the problem that the customer is experiencing we need to listen to the customer. So many times I have experienced people interrupting me while I am trying to explain to them what had happened. It frustrates me; they can't let me talk just for two minutes. And usually I was trying to one understand the question or second explaining what happened and what to do about it. And again some people are a lot better at listening and solving problems, but I think that this is something that can be developed. We can develop that listening ear, what to listen to, and how to interperate what is being said. Of course it is one of those things that requires a lot of practice.

Another aspect of banking that makes it unique is the information that is required by the bank. If you are applying for a loan you have to provide some pretty personal information: tax returns, investment accounts statements, credit report. These pieces of information are items that people tend not to talk about a lot in front of other people. In fact the bank takes it very serious and they have privacy disclosures that are passed out with every new account and loan that is opened. It lets you know that we will not sell any of your information or share anything with anyone but you. People have been fired over this issue, because they go out and tell someone about someone else's finances.

Thinking about this, when we are trying to witness and share Jesus with people. We are really building a unique relationship with these people. It's a relationship that most people don't experience. Hopefully it is a relationship that we can share our deepest fears and regrets, along with our dreams, without having to worry about getting laughed at in the process. God is kind of like the personal information that the bank gets for the new accounts opened. And sometimes we have those people that open up right away and then we have those that take a long time and a lot of work to get to talk.

And we have to stick with it. And be there with a listening ear for others. We all have family to get home to, or a movie to catch, or email to check. We always feel that we need to be moving. I really struggle with this. Sometimes we just have to take a couple of minutes and give someone a call. Just to check up on them. It is amazing how much a simple phone call can affect people. It's saying, hey I really do care for you. Or having a piece of pie with someone. I really believe that it is hard to find someone to really listen to you. And I think as Christians we need to train ourselves to be different. Jesus tells us, "everyone should be quick to listen, slow to speak and slow to become angry" (James 1:19). I really believe that when we listen it really sets us apart from the world. And I have often listened to people but have had no idea what to say afterwards. But you know that God has always been faithful. He has done a combination of two things. First off, I believe that He has given me the words to speak to that person. Lets look at Paul's request in Ephesians: "Pray also for me, that whenever I open my mouth, words may be given me so that I will fearlessly make known the mystery of the gospel" (Ephesians 6:19). So if Paul is praying that prayer, why can't we? Second it just helps. They are able to feel better having someone listen to them and hear them self talk through it out loud. One thing that I have learned is not to be scared of silence. Especially in certain situations, it might take people longer to warm up and want to talk things through. We have to build up trust with that person. At first I think we have to encourage them to open up, and once they do it helps them out.

Sometimes it takes more than just listening to people, we need to take action. If it causes us to sin or go against another brother we shouldn't do it. "If someone forces you to go one mile, go with him two miles. Give to the one who asks you, and do not turn away from the one who wants to borrow from you" (Matthew 5:41-42).

In any line of business people know what their competitors are. For instance when the bank down the street has a CD special, we make it a point to know the terms of that special. And we react to the special accordingly. Same thing with religion, there are a lot of other religions out there. They are a lot more complicated than Christianity. To put it plainly in Christianity Jesus died for us, it is done, and we just have to receive the grace of Jesus Christ. Where in other religions we have to pray so many times, or make a long journey, or even sacrifice our bodies. Again it is not necessarily that we are selling Christ, but it might not hurt us to investigate a little bit about other religions so we are not ignorant to them. Sometimes if we have a better understanding about the different religions we will be able to reach out better to those people.

I think that a lot of times we even forget about the religion of money and materialism. We are so worried about Islam, Buddhism, etc. that we forget about the idols that we make in our own culture. There are many people trapped in those. "No one can serve two masters. Either he will hate the one and love the other, or he will be devoted to the one and despise the other. You cannot serve both God and Money" (Matthew 6:24).

Retirement Plans

*"Our home is in Heaven where we eagerly await
a savior from there, Jesus Christ".*
Philippians 3:20

If you turn on the radio or the TV, or if you even just look into the newspaper you are going to see add after add about retirement planning. Whether it is about a 401K plan or IRA, or even just a consultant about planning on saving for retirement.

It's such a hot topic that the government is trying to encourage people to save for their retirements through tax savings on investment decisions like IRA and ROTH IRAs. They are also trying to encourage people to save by bumping up the maximum amount that people can put into their IRAs. Along with the catch up policy, that allows people to put in even more money if you are a certain age.

Coming out of college thinking of retirement was one of the last things that was on my mind. I am going to have to work many years before I will reach that level. So many people are like me. That they feel retirement is so far away. They don't realize the importance of saving money today and investing it in the long haul. Instead we start families, and of course we have to have that new car or that new house. So we are spending a lot of money on all of these and other things but we are not saving. And then forty years down the line when we reach retirement, depending on if the government changes any laws about retirement. We don't have as much money as we need to live off of. In fact, the national papers have articles all the time, "more than half of paid workers 25 to 64 don't have retirement savings accounts of any kind. About a third work for employers who don't offer retirement benefits, a congressional study."[viii] There are so many articles now in the paper about social security and how much money we need to retire with. It is a major problem in America, especially for the baby boomers. "Our savings rates here are a disaster, and the study continues to beat home the crisis in savings overall,"[ix] said Derrick Max. So of course our human nature kicks in. We start to worry. And of course that gets us nowhere. People half jokingly talk about how they will have to work till they drop or that they might have to find part time jobs. That they might not be able to travel all over the world or be able to play golf five times a week.

We as Christians are still concerned about some of these things. However our real retirement doesn't start at 59.5 year old. It starts when Jesus comes again and takes us home. "Our home is in Heaven where we eagerly await a savior from there, Jesus Christ"(Philippians 3:20). And throughout the New Testament we are told that Heaven is a beautiful place. It is a place where we will not be disappointed Jesus tells us that there are many rooms in his father's house and he is preparing a room for us. We will not have to worry if we have enough money to make it through our earthly retirement, or if we have enough money to cover the nursing home bills.

And since we don't have to worry and since we can go into retirement at any time shouldn't we make the most of each day. Jesus tells us, who of you by worrying can add a single hour to his life" (Matthew 6:27)? And we are also told in the Psalms, "You have made my days a mere handbreadth; the span of my years is as nothing before you. Each man's life is but a breath" (Psalm 39:5). So we need to go out there and make a difference and live each day to the fullest. "Be very careful, then, how you live – not as unwise but as wise, making the most of every opportunity, because the days are evil" (Ephesians 5:15-16). Colossians has a similar message, "Be wise in the way you act toward outsiders; make the most of every opportunity. Let your conversation is always full of grace, seasoned with salt, so that you may know how to answer everyone" (Colossians 4:5-6). We find numerous verses on this, it must have been very important to Christ.

Let us not forget the importance of giving to kingdom purposes. The Churches, radio station, missionaries all need funds to operate. We should be obedient and give of our money. And time after all God is the one that has blessed us with the job that we have, along with the salary. "Do not store up for you treasures on earth, where moth and rust destroy, and where thieves break in and steal. But store up for yourselves treasures in heaven, where moth and rust do not destroy and where thieves do not break in and steal" (Matthew 6:19-20). It is guaranteed to be there, its not going anywhere. "So do not throw away your confidence; it will be richly rewarded. You need to persevere so that when you have done the will of God, you will receive what he has promised" (Hebrews 10:35-36).

Then just as people have big retirement parties when they reach retirement, shouldn't we also rejoice when the Lord calls us home. Its hard seeing our loved ones pass. But isn't reassuring that they are in no more pain or troubles of this world. If we are all believers we will see those people again. And they are in a much better place.

We must also remember that we brought nothing into this world and we can take nothing out of it. "But godliness with contentment is great gain. For we brought nothing into the world, and we can take nothing out of it. But if we have food and clothing, we will be content with that. People who want to get rich fall into temptation and a trap and into many foolish and harmful desires that plunge men into ruin and destruction. For the love of money is a root of all kinds of evil. Some people, eager for money, have wandered from the faith and pierced themselves with many grief" (1Timothy 6:6-10). And we always want more and more stuff. Its our human nature. Why, we are not going to be able to take it with us. I am sure that you have heard that saying that you have never seen a hearse with a u-haul behind it. "So we fix our eyes not on what is seen, but on what is unseen. For what is seen is temporary, but what is unseen is eternal" (2 Corinthians 4:18). So we need to stop running after those things and store up treasures in heaven instead. We are wasting our time with chasing after those things. And we are warned about losing things that we have given up for Christ. "Watch out that you do not lose what you have worked for, but that you may be rewarded fully" (2 John 1:8).

We Need to be Examples

"In everything set them an example by doing what is good".

Titus 2:7

We as Christians have to realize that we are suppose to set an example for all of the non-believers. And I think that our Savior, Jesus Christ, gave us a perfect example. He told us not to sin, and guess what, He didn't sin. He put his words into action, it was not do as I say and not what I do, but do as I do. "In everything set them an example by doing what is good. In your teaching show integrity, seriousness and soundness of speech that cannot be condemned, so that those who oppose you may be ashamed because they have nothing bad to say about us" (Titus 2:7-8). Not always an easy way to live. I feel that sometimes we are really let down by people around us because they do tell us one thing and then do the opposite. These people might be our best friends, spouse, parents, boss, or pastors.

I think that if we set examples and live our lives as Christ calls us to. People will really be attracted to us. We are told that if we follows God's will that He will bless us and gives us much fruit. "I am the vine; you are the branches. If a man remains in me and I in him, he will bear much fruit; apart from me you can do nothing" (John 15:5). And I think that if we truly live our lives for Christ, it is pretty attractive from a non-Christian's point of view. We are living for an external purpose, not just for ourselves. And not so much, that if we follow God's will, that we will be millionaires, but things just seem to fall into place. It's because we put our trust into Christ so He is going to be faithful and provide for us every-day. "And why do you worry about clothes? See how the lilies of the field grow. They do not labor or spin. Yet I tell you that not even Solomon in all his splendor was dressed like one of these. If that is how God clothes the grass of the field, which is here today and tomorrow is thrown into the fire, will he not much clothe you, O you of little faith? So do not worry, saying, 'What shall we eat?' or 'What shall we drink?' or 'What shall we wear?' For the pagans run after all these things, and your heavenly Father knows that you need them. But seek first his kingdom and his righteousness, and all these things will be given you as well" (Matthew 6:28-33). God is going to provide for us, He says so Himself.

But I think that leading by example also gains respect from others. If we tell others that they are suppose to live this way and this way, we better be ready to the same thing. We should never ask someone to do something we person-ally wouldn't do. It will also help us to relate to one another and talk about what is going on in their lives. We will also have respect the people around us. The changes that they have to go through to change to live how Christ calls them to live. "For we do not have a high priest who is unable to sympathize with our weaknesses, but we have one who has been tempted in every way, just as we are – yet was without sin. Let us then approach the throne of grace with confidence, so that we may receive mercy and find grace to help us in our time of need" (Hebrews 4:15-16). No one likes to follow a hyprocrite. No one likes to follow someone who has no compassion. So even if we live our lives the way we believe without compromising with integrity we should earn the respect of our non-Christian co-workers or friends.

I think that a big area in which we are challenged to set an example is with our tongue. We are told that the tongue is a very powerful thing; you can either degrade people or make them feel like nothing, or use it and just build people up. "With the tongue we praise our Lord and Father, and with it we curse men, who have been made in God's likeness. Out of the same mouth come praise and cursing. My brothers, this should not be" (James 3:9-10). It is sad how true this is. I can get into a big verbal fight right before church. And then when I come to church I can sing and praise God like nothing ever happened. There is something wrong with that picture.

Some ways I think that we can improve in this area is by not wanting to argue. I know that some people like to argue, and the Bible has something to say about that, "he who loves a quarrel loves sin" (Proverbs 17:19). "And the Lord's servant must not quarrel; instead he must be kind to everyone, able to teach, not resentful" (2 Timothy 2:24). "Starting a quarrel is like breaching a dam; so drop the matter before a dispute breaks out" (Proverbs 17:14). "Do everything without complaining or arguing, so that you may become blameless and pure, children of God without fault in a crooked and depraved generation, in which you shine like stars in the universe as you hold out the word of life – in order that I may boast on the day of Christ that I did not run or labor for nothing" (Philippians 2:14-16). Here are four verses that explain why quarreling is so dangerous for us as a believer. And in our quarreling and complaining we end up saying a lot of things that we don't mean and we wish we could take back. Which hurts our integrity with other people. And of course when we lose that respect it takes a long time to regain it, a lot longer than it takes to lose it. "But I tell you that men will have to give account on the day of judgment for every careless word they have spoken. For by your words you will be acquitted, and by your words you will be condemned" (Matthew 12:36-37). Wow, so let us truly think before we speak. That kind of hurts, every word we are going to be accountable for. "For everyone looks out for his own interests, not of Jesus Christ" (Philippians 2:21). I believe that these are some building blocks, which are principles in the Bible. And if we desire to change I assure you it will not be easy and an overnight process. It is something that we need to continue to work at.

I know that it's not an easy thing, especially depending on the certain people you are in contact with. But I believe that if we can hold our tongue and not jump to conclusions it will help us witness to others. We truly have to think before we speak. We need to think whether or not what we are going to say is going to build someone up. If it is glorifying Christ Jesus. If not we should not say it.

Some other ways that we can set examples for others are: "Let your gentleness be evident to all. The Lord is near" (Philippians 4:5). Gentle according to Webster's dictionary, is "generous, kind, patient." But then if you look at the fruits of the spirit which is talked about in Galatians "But the fruit of the spirit is love, joy, peace, patience, kindness, goodness, faithfulness, gentleness and self control" (Galatians 5:22). If we live with these aspects in our live we will set ourselves apart from the world, for the world to see how Christ is living in us. "A new command I give you: Love one another. As I have loved you, so you must love one another. By this all men will know that you are my disciples, if you love on another," (John 13:34-35).

The Bible and Jesus really talks about love. I personally think that in our generation the word is over used and kind of watered down. But looking at Webster love is: "a feeling of brotherhood and good will toward other people."[x] We are told in the Bible what love is, "This is how we know what love is: Jesus Christ laid down his life for us. And we ought to lay down our lives for our brothers" (1 John 3:16). Or we can look at 1 Corinthians, "Love is patient, love is kind. It does not envy, it does not boast, it is not proud. It is not rude, it is not self-seeking, it is not easily angered, it keeps no record of wrongs. Love does not delight in evil but rejoices with the truth" (1 Corinthians 13:4). So we are suppose to love one another, this is suppose to set us apart from others. "Therefore, although in Christ I could be bold and order you to do what you ought to do, yet I appeal to you on the basis of love" (Philemon 1:8-9).

The fruits of the spirit are hard to live by twenty-four seven. However we never know who is watching and what kind of impact that it is going to have on those people watching. So we have to do our best, we just need to take it one minute at a time. If we try to look at a whole year or month at a time we will feel overwhelmed. And if we feel weak we should pray for strength. God will surely give it to us.

Can't Overlook People

"They only heard the report: 'the man who formerly persecuted us is now preaching the faith he once tried to destroy'".

Galatians 1:23

When I had graduated college and started working, I started to look for a car to buy. Well needless to say I didn't take my dad along all the time. Besides it was I buying the car not him, and I wanted the salesman to talk to me and not him. Well being a young and well-educated young man I had a pretty good idea on what kind of car I wanted so I went a head and went to the appropriate dealerships. I do have to say at most of the dealerships I was disappointed because a lot of the salesmen were not willing to work with me. So obviously I did not purchase the car from any of those dealerships. And it was getting pretty discouraging from my standpoint. But I guess if you look long and hard enough you eventually find what you are looking for. I found a wonderful salesman that was willing to work with me. And he found what I was looking for.

I felt that I was overlooked and not taken seriously because of my age. And I will tell you one thing, I will not go back to some of those dealerships. Am I being maybe a little harsh? I don't know. I personally hope that I will not have to buy another car for a while, because of my experiences.

We as Christians probably act the same way. We probably think that someone would never give his or her life to Christ. For a number of reasons, maybe because of their age, or their life style, or social class, or race, the list of excuses can go on an on. I know I have done this were I don't talk to someone because I don't feel that they are interested in Christ. Most of time I just look at people, and because the way they are dressed or carry themselves. I figure they are the least bit interested, what a shame on my part. Well I got a big slap in the face. I went away to school right, well I come back and started helping out around church and I noticed this other guy about my age, he looked pretty familiar. So after a while I kind of placed him and asked him when he graduated and where he went to High school. And sure enough I knew of him, but because I was a goodie Christian I didn't bother to talk to him because I figured since he dressed a little different and listened to different music he was not interested in Christ. Well while I was gone at college someone invested into him and now he is living his life for Christ. And what a man of faith he has become. It is amazing how he had encouraged me in my own walk. Here I am a few years earlier thinking that there is no way he would be interested in Christ and why would I waste my precious time talking to him then. What a lie Satan tells us. Sometimes I feel that I think too much, I just have to have to take that step of faith. I have to trust God.

"They only heard the report: 'the man who formerly persecuted us is now preaching the faith he once tried to destroy.' And they praised God because of me" (Galatians

1:23-24), which Paul is talking about himself. Here these tax guys were there telling people that they need to stone Stephen, in Acts. Which he was the first martyr after Christ. Which at that time Paul's name was Saul. But God used this person to write most of the New Testament. He was broken and then gave himself fully to Christ. And look at how Christ used him. So let us not count people out for Christ's sake. "I became a servant of this gospel by the gift of God's grace given me through the working of his power. Although I am the less than the least of all God's people, this grace was given me: to preach to the Gentiles the unsearchable riches of Christ, and to make plain to everyone the administration of this mystery, which for the ages past was kept hidden in God, who created all things" (Ephesians 3:7-9). Listen to Paul again: "I thank Christ Jesus our Lord, who has given me strength, that he considered me faithful, appointing me to his service. Even though I was once a blasphemer and a persecutor and a violent man, I was shown mercy because I acted in ignorance and unbelief. The grace of our Lord was poured out on me abundantly, along with faith and love that are in Christ Jesus. Here is a trustworthy saying that deserves full acceptance: Christ Jesus came into the world to save sinners – of whom I am the worst. But for that very reason I was shown mercy so that in me, the worst of sinners, Christ Jesus might display his unlimited patience as an example for those who would believe on him and receive eternal life. Now to the King eternal, immortal, invisible, the only God, be honor and glory for ever and ever, Amen" (1 Timothy 1:12-17). Paul knows that he is undeserving. He is completely humble, Paul totally gives God all the credit, it was nothing that Paul did, and it was all God. But if you think about it. We are all in the same boat. Without Grace there is no chance for us.

We are told about the Beatitudes. These are God's people.

"Now when he saw the crowds, he went up on a mountainside and sat down. His disciples came to him, and he began to teach them, saying: 'blessed are the poor in spirit, for theirs is the kingdom of heaven. Blessed are those who mourn, for they will be comforted. Blessed are the meek, for they will inherit the earth. Blessed are those who hunger and thirst for righteousness, for they will be filled. Blessed are the merciful, for they will be shown mercy. Blessed are the pure in heart, for they will see God. Blessed are the peacemakers, for they will be called sons of God. Blessed are those who are persecuted because of righteous-ness, for theirs is the kingdom of heaven. Blessed are you when people insult you, persecute you and falsely say all kinds of evil against you because of me. Rejoice and be glad, because great is your reward in heaven, for in the same way they persecuted the prophets who were before you".

(Matthew 5:1-12)

We also can't rule out the uneducated. First of all God says that the wisdom of this world is foolish. But even look at the people he surrounded himself with. All of the disciples were uneducated, a couple were fishermen. Nothing wrong with that but they were no Pharisees. The Pharisees knew the law inside and out, but they became to legalistic. They had no love, they were very judgmental. But Jesus' disciples were genuine. They didn't get caught up in all of the laws and legalism.

We as Christians have to reach out to everyone. We should not exclude anyone. I realize that it is a lot easier said than done. But we have to show everyone Christ's love and compassion. And we must remember that, if they reject Christ and they are not rejecting us. It's really Christ they are rejecting, not us. But we don't know maybe you might be the only Christian to come in contact with them. We don't know what kind of seeds we are sowing. We have to take that chance on someone; someone did it for us right? Time for us to return the favor. And who knows maybe we will hit a home run. I know a lot of people that were not really looking for God. But God used other people in their lives to draw them to himself.

Being Careful

"Do not give the devil a foothold".

Ephesians 4:27

We cannot underestimate how we impact people. Especially each other. Again going through my rotation I had met people of all walks of life. I was pretty excited about going into this department because I know that one of the employees was a Christian. Unfortunately it didn't turn out to be exactly what I pictured it to be. Usually that is the case, I tend to I have high expectations and besides Christ they are rarely met. Its just human nature if we put our expectations and trust in people we will eventually be let down by them. Which I think is okay in the long run, because it reminds me time and time again not to put my faith in people but in God. I also want to say that I know that I am not perfect and unfortunately I have let lots of other people down. However God still decides to use my fellow co-worker and myself, it's a mystery.

I recall this one day we were working together. He had received some pocket calendars from one of his clients. These calendars were not exactly Christian calendars;

they had pictures of women with barely any clothing covering them. Like I said he had a couple of them so he offered one to me and I just kind of blew it off and said 'no' a few times. He insisted so instead of making a big scene I just decided to take it and be done with it. But what is this Christian man giving me another Christian, which we have talked about the churches we attend, giving me this swimsuit calendar. And maybe some of you don't think that there is any harm to all of this. But I believe that it is giving the devil a foot hold, "do not give the devil a foothold" (Ephesians 4:27).

At the time I was given the calendar I had had a rough day. Problems with the computer at work, just being tired which resulted in having my guard down. And guess what, I did give the devil a foothold. The devil knows are weaknesses all to well. And he is going to go after us with all he has, even if it is using other Christians against us. It might not always be a swimsuit calendar, but maybe it is our attitude or our language or how we dress. Which of course we don't always know this, that the devil is using us to bring down others. And I am sure that if we knew the devil was using us we would stop everything that we were doing. So after work and doing a little bit of running around I felt that it was time to relax so I decided to rent a movie. The movie I had rented was rated R and had some sexual material in the movie, which again caused me to stumble. Causing me to have impure thoughts. I had picked the movie because the story line was okay and because I had heard that there was some sexual content in the movie.

Lust and impure thoughts are something that I have struggled with a long time and continue to struggle with. Some days are better than others. The devil just caught me at a bad time, a good time for the devil. Like I said I was having a rough day things were not going as I had planned. Which makes for a good time for Satan to make me stumble, at a time that I was weak and my guard was down.

Now I shouldn't blame my fellow co-worker who is a believer. He didn't know what areas I struggle in. But it was myself that drove to the video store, who picked out the movie, and who watched the movie. There were plenty of things that I could have done to prevent myself from watching the movie. However, if I didn't even see that calendar earlier in the day maybe things might have been different. Maybe the devil would not of have that foot hole that he did. And of course if the calendar failed, the devil has plenty of others ways to try to get me to fall.

There is another passage in the Bible, "So whether you eat or drink or whatever you do, do it all for the glory of God. Do not cause anyone to stumble, whether Jews, Greeks or the church of God – even as I try to please everybody in every way. For I am not seeking my own good but the good of many, so that they may be saved" (1 Corinthians 10:31-33). It would be horrible to do something to make another person stumble. "You were running a good race. Who cut in on you and kept you from obeying the truth? That kind of persuasion does not come from the one who calls you. 'A little yeast works through the whole batch of dough.' I am confident in the Lord that you will take no other view. The one who is throwing you into confusion will pay the penalty, whoever he may be" (Galatians 5:7-10). And some things are going to be more cut and dry than others. I personally however don't want that responsibility of cutting in on someone while they are running their race.

So hopefully we can keep that in mind more. Maybe when you are eating lunch with fellow employees you don't tell those jokes you heard last night. Or if they are gossiping about the new employee, you don't join in the conversation. You could say something about R-rated movies. Some people don't believe seeing them, and God bless them. But if you want to go see a movie, and bring another believer with you. That other believer might struggle with impure thoughts or with their language. We need to be concerned about these things. So seeing some of those movies out there today are not going to help them. Some people believe that it is okay to have some alcohol at dinner, which is totally between them and God. But if you know that the people you are with have struggled with alcohol before I pray that you will not drink in front of them. Which might cause them to order some in which they might be too much for them to handle. We know that Jesus doesn't condemn alcohol but there are also plenty of warnings about it. Each case is different. I also hope that you and I would never do anything against God's will. If we are causing someone to stumble hopefully that person will let us know. Hopefully we would do the same, by telling the person who is causing us to stumble. We should not get offensive if someone approaches us about something that causes him or her to stumble. Let's not forget that we are working all on the same team.

No Loyalty

"When evening came, the owner of the vineyard said to his foreman, 'Call the workers and pay them their wages, beginning with the last ones hired and going on to the first'".

Matthew 20:8

Again with the position that I was given I was able to go around meeting all kinds of people. And believe it or not some of those people didn't particularly like there jobs. So of course they didn't have the greatest things to say about the company. The common complaint about the company is that they doesn't care about the employee, they just care about the bottom line. That companies are not what they use to be, where they would have employees for twenty, thirty years; there is no more loyalty to the employees. And of course if you talk to the president and CEOs, in their eyes the employees have no loyalty to the company, because if they get a job offer somewhere else for more money. Off the employee goes. So it is a two way street and we will leave it at that. But I do think that there is some truth to both sides of the coin.

First off if we Christians are complaining which is not setting a great example. God calls us to: "Do everything without complaining or arguing, so that you may become blameless and pure, children of God without fault in a crooked and depraved generation, in which you shine like stars in the universe as you hold out the word of life" (Philippians 2:14-16). I realize that some of our jobs we can't particularly enjoy and it is easy to complain. We have to remember that we are representing Jesus Christ in our work place. If we are obedient to God, He will provide for us.

There were a couple of people that told me to always have my resume updated and ready to hand out. To always keep my eyes up for something else. And again I do think that there is some logic to that. I also firmly believe as a Christian, and especially if we are praying about our future, that God is going to provide for us. I believe that God will make it known when we, if we are supposed to, make a job change. I have kind of realized that some of these people that were so vocal about how they are not happy at work, are the same ones that are always complaining about their goals, and their hours. They feel that they are not being recognized.

We as for being a Christian we have to remember that we need to stand our ground. And sure God might call us to different companies or jobs. But as Christians we need to stand tall. If we feel that we are not being recognized in our Christian efforts, we should not explore different religions. That's foolish. "Am I now trying to win the approval of men, or of God? Or am I trying to please men, I would not be a servant of Christ" (Galatians 1:10). Or even if we are in a valley of our walk with God, we just have to tough it out. Again not everything in life is going to be easy. Jesus tells us that we are going to have a hard life. But God promises to be with us. It is very short life in comparison to eternity, lets us remember that. Also, I think that sometimes we learn and grow the most in those tough times. "I have told you these things, so that in me you may have peace. In this world you will have trouble. But take heart! I have overcome the world" (John 16:33).

Again in the Christian walk of life, years don't matter to God. We are the same if we have been following Christ for 20 years or just 2. We can look at the parable of the Workers in the Vineyard found in Matthew 20. Those people that started working in the field first thing are those people that have been following Christ for 20 plus years. And those obviously who came in the late afternoon, which received the same reward, are those who have only been following Christ for a year or two. The important thing is once we give our lives to Christ, we are to stay on that straight and narrow, which He calls us to.

So let us remember even thought there might not be loyalty among our companies and employees. There is loyalty between Christ and His children. God might provide us other ways to serve Him, and that is great. As long as we remember it is all about Christ. And for us Christians that should be our bottom line, that's what we should always have in sight.

No Trust

"I tell you the truth, anyone who has faith in me will do what I have been doing. He will do even greater things than these, because I am going to the Father".

John 14:12

Another thing that I have heard throughout my rotation is not to trust anyone. I have heard that I should document everything that I do, phone conversations, transfers, whatever I do. The reason why is, if something goes wrong. No one is going to stick up for you. That they are going to leave you out to dry all by yourself. And I did notice that, people would ask others to do something for them. When people want some account updates on their account and they would ask for it over the phone. Most of time the person that was doing the transaction will ask for a email, describing exactly what they want done. It's a great idea. Because when they print out that email, it has the time, date, what is supposed to be done, and who it was sent by. And I have seen the benefits of documenting everything that you have done, because it is true, if something goes wrong very few people will stick up for you.

It is a sad world that we live in. If you look in the paper someone is always suing someone else for something. And the Bible talks about that a little bit. "And if someone wants to sue you and take your tunic, let him have your cloak as well" (Matthew 5:40). Some people are out to get others any way they can. So I am not saying that we shouldn't document and be professional. We should that way no one can question our work. But in the kingdom it's going to be different. A handshake will mean something again. When we give our word, we should mean it, not just blowing steam. "Simply let your 'Yes' be 'Yes,' and your 'No', 'No'; anything beyond this comes from the evil one" (Matthew 5:37).

Another thing that I realize that often happens in life is talking about people behind their backs. That there is no trust between employees because they have heard that they have talked about them behind their backs, saying this and that. And I have been there, both sides of the coin. It can be so easy to join in a conversation when they are talking about someone else. And sure enough it stings pretty bad when you hear people talking about you.

During my rotation I was working in one of the branches where they had several departments. Well I was informed that one of the ladies in another department was talking bad about me. Now I didn't even know her. But I guess that she had a problem with the bank hiring me and putting me through this training program. I admit that sometimes it is hard to justify putting people through extensive training programs. Not everyone understands the concept. So I guess she was saying that I must have been related to someone in upper management and that I needed a job. And that they created a position and just gave it to me. Which did not sit to well with me. Well a few months later I was going to work in her department, of course still remembering it. I prayed about it, and sure enough God answered my prayers. She was really nice to me. She actually took me under her wing. Unfortunately not every story ends up that way. I have learned to stay away from a couple of people. And my reasoning is sometimes it is just better to avoid those conflicts. If God has something in store for me, maybe something to say to that person later on than so be it. We have to be open to God working through us. That is why God says pray for our enemies. "But I tell you: Love your enemies and pray for those who persecute you, that you may be sons of your Father in heaven. He causes his sun to rise on the evil and the good, and sends rain on the righteous and the unrighteous" (Matthew 5:44-45). We have to be determined to be showing these people love.

We also have to remember that people talked behind Jesus' back. Of course they made up that charges that they charged him with. "The chief priests and the whole Sanhedrin were looking for false evidence against Jesus so that they could put him to death. But they did not find any, though many false witnesses came forward" (Matthew 26:59). Here is a perfect and blameless person, it's Jesus. They didn't have any dirt on Him, they simply didn't like Him. Of course they had to make up stuff. "Finally two came forward and declared, "This fellow said, ' I am able to destroy the temple of God and rebuild it in three days'" (Matthew 26:61). And look at how Jesus handled it. He was very professional. He didn't throw mud back at them. Jesus went in peace, He even restored one of the soldiers' ear.

So as Christians we have to remember a few things. The first one is that when people are talking about others, we should not participate in those conversations. Even if that means leaving the room. Another thing is we should not let this bother you. I know that it is easier said that done. It's not always easy to hear people make acqutions about you.

But in a way we should feel honored that they have nothing better to talk about than us. As Christians we need to realize that people are watching us, I have heard that we have a bull's eye on the back of us. We need to live our lives the way Christ calls us to live. If we do that people are going to notice us. They noticed Jesus didn't they, and "I tell you the truth, anyone who has faith in me will do what I have been doing. He will do even greater things than these, because I am going to the Father" (John 14:12). So we should not get caught up in pleasing people, but God. We will never be able to please everyone.

Being People of Our Word

"Simply let your 'Yes' be 'Yes' and your 'No,' 'No'; anything beyond this comes from the evil one".

Matthew 5:37

We have to remember that people are watching us. They are watching us to see why we are different, what makes us different. They also want to see how we are living our lives, since we call ourselves Christians. They want to know if its just a name or a way of life. Some may want to see if they can trip us up, if they can make us stumble. They may feel intimidated when we are around them or just plainly feel uncomfortable around us. Some people react differently when they are around Christians.

We as Christians have to realize how important our words are. There are a lot of times that we just let our mouths do the talking with out even thinking about it. We say anything to close the deal or to get someone off of our back. We will give any excuses why we didn't hit our goals. Why we didn't close the deal or why we were late. We have to make sure that we are telling the truth. That will add to our testimony. That will again give us credibility and integrity.

Again I was working in the trades for a while. It was kind of slow point so we were doing some residential, friends of the owners. So I talked to the owner of the company the day before to get directions and all of the low down on the project. Well that first day, I was late. I had written down the wrong street. Knowing that I was lost, I tried to get a hold of him, but couldn't. So I called the office. Fortunately they could help me out. So when I got to the house, my boss was there. Which was pretty typical especially being a friend of his and to start us out. So right away I apologized for being late and explained how I wrote down the wrong address. He told me that it was no big deal that it happens. Just don't let it happen again. Well come to find out after he left the guy I was working with was giving me grief. I guess the boss was worried about me. The reason being is because I was always on the job site on time and if I was late I was always up front with him.

Now I could have got out of the car and told him that you know everyone else is late and I deserve a chance to be late. And start pointing fingers and making excuses. Or I could have told him that he gave me the wrong directions. But that would have gotten me nowhere. In fact I probably would have ended up worse than I did. And maybe there might be some months that you don't meet your sales goals or your benchmarks or you could not complete all your work in time. I encourage you as Christians to be honest why you were off this month or quarter. Of course some people aren't going to be pleased but there is nothing you can do about it, especially as long as you did your best. In the Bible it tells us, "simply let your 'Yes' be 'Yes,' and your 'No', 'No'; anything beyond this comes from the evil one" (Matthew 5:37). Some quarters are going to be tougher than others. You can't help that, but be honest with yourself and your boss.

And that goes for everything. If you receive a question that you don't know. Don't say something just to say it. Be honest with the employee or customer. I think that they will really respect that. And you aren't off the hook yet. Go find the answer for your customer and yourself to know in the future.

I think that also sometimes we try to sugar coat things. We need to stop that and be straight forward with people. If people are going to get a higher price, tell them that. Same thing with Christianity if people are leading a sinful life and they need to change their ways. We need to tell those people. Yes it is not easy, and we are not sure how they are going to react. But we need to do it out of love. We have to stop fooling ourselves that everything is going to be okay. To just give it time to work itself out. Remember we are not guaranteed tomorrow; let's live each day to the fullest.

Before and even now I still struggle, but I am very hard on people, especially with family members. I think part of it is that I have such high expectations. Another area in my life, which I would like to think that I am getting better at is the whole money thing. I constantly worried about money. I was wondering how I could always make an extra buck or two. And again I still struggle, but I think that the Lord has taught me not to put my trust into money. My negative attitude has to stop also. It is always easy to look at the bad stuff, the stuff that is always going wrong. Which also causes me say things that I really didn't mean and could not take back. In order to me more like Jesus I had to change that, He looks at me and He sees this beautiful creation and longs to have a relationship with this no good, messed up guy.

"A man of knowledge uses words with restraint, and a man of understanding is even-tempered. Even a fool is thought wise if he keeps silent, and discerning if he holds his tongue" (Proverbs 17:27-28). Here this Proverb tells us that we should use our words sparingly, that we should not go out there and just run our mouths. "When words are many, sin is not absent, but he who holds his tongue is wise" (Proverbs 10:19). I find this to be so true. The more that I talk and try to swing a deal the deeper and deeper I am digging myself into a hole. When I was late if I would have tried to blame traffic, or directions, I could have ended up getting in a lot more trouble. I would have done the classic foot in mouth syndrome.

"Do not let any unwholesome talk come out of your mouths, but only what is helpful for building others up according to their needs, that it may benefit those who listen" (Ephesians 4:29). I am sure that we all have heard the phrase, don't say nothing if you can't say anything nice at all. That's what God is saying. What kind of a witness does that show if we are always ripping on people? Besides if no one else is around God is not about that, He is about love. We do not know who is listening in on our conversation. Maybe we are in cubical, it can be very easy to over hear conversation, or at lunch. With the same mouth you curse man and praise God. That's not right, lets really make an effort to remember that.

Our mouth is a very powerful thing. Which is often misused and not taken care of. "When we put bits into the mouths of horses to make them obey us, we can turn the whole animal. Or take ships as an example. Although they are so large and are driven by strong winds, they are steered by a very small rudder wherever the pilot wants to go. Likewise the tongue is a small part of the body, but it makes great boasts. Consider when a great forest is set on fire by a small spark. The tongue also is a fire, a world of evil among the parts of the body. It corrupts the whole person, sets the whole course of his life on fire, and is itself set on fire by hell," (James 3:3-6). It's not a easy thing to change. But if we spend time praying about it, as well as becoming more conscience what we are saying. These are two big steps in managing our mouth and what comes out of it. We have to be intentional about changing.

The Power of Gathering Together, being Visible

"Let us not give up meeting together, as some are in the habit of doing, but let us encourage one another – and all the more as you see the Day approaching".

Hebrews 10:25

Jesus told us "if two of you on earth agree about anything you ask for, it will be done for you by my Father in heaven. For where two or three come together in my name, there am I with them" (Matthew 18:19-20). There are many times that I have been encouraged and have really felt the Holy Spirit when I have gathered with other Christians. To be honest a lot of that had happened when I was still in school. However I really have not experienced this so much at work, which is partly my fault. For instance each year in the fall was 'see you at the pole'. It always amazed me how many people would come out to that, and especially some of the individuals. Usually the time of prayer was really good, however I was always excited to see who was there. Then throughout the day when I saw the individuals I approached them or they approached myself and it was so awesome just to be able to talk. Especially talk about Christ. We had a special bond; we were brothers and sisters in Christ. In the same way it was kind of sad because if we were Christians and others didn't realize it, are we doing something wrong? I know that for me I am very shy about my faith. If someone asks me, I will probably tell him or her that I go to church. I won't really tell them that I am living for Jesus and that He is my personal Lord and Savior and how he is presently working in my life. I'll take the wimpy way out.

Like I said I am pretty passive in this area, about approaching other people about their faiths. Unless it is an organized event, other people have to approach me about my faith. Which I feel more comfortable about since they are approaching me. They may be asking the questions. However what happens when there are two passive people like myself in the same company. Which we both have a passion for prayer or a heart for our fellow employees. We are never going to be able to make that connection. We are not going to be able to encourage each other or pray for each other effectively. That is something that I need to personally work on, being a little more proactive. It's like running a generator but not using all the power and letting most of the electricity go to waste. I have to realize that there is power when we gather. And if we don't get together we are not tapping into all of God's power.

I believe that there is a lot of power in praying together. For instance the 'see you at the pole'. We all went to the same college, so most of us knew the needs of the college. We had that common ground to build off of. God might give a certain individual something to pray and when we hear that prayer a light goes on in our head. I might know what professor they are praying for and I might not have known that he was sick. I became aware of a lot more that was going on around campus because others were praying about those situations. Also within our companies you will know different people in your department than I will. That way we can pray for the people and the company more effectively. I learned the needs of different schools or departments, different ministries on campus, the different dorms, etc.

Maybe for your company you might have a group of three that decides to pray for your company once a week. Well one person might be in the sales force, while another one might be the accountant, and another might be in customer service. Now I know that some things have to be kept secret till the right time. And you should not abuse your fellow brothers and sisters in Christ trying to get information from them. But the salesperson should know that if numbers are down or a big sales meeting coming up, that is something that you can lay before the Lord. The accountant would know if there is a big audit that is taking place. And these prayers can be very general and generic; God knows what we mean, even when we don't know completely. He is just pleased that we are taking time out of our day, to gather with some co-workers and pray.

Again I think that coming together and reading scriptures has power. There are a lot of times that I read scripture and I don't know exactly what it is about so I skip over it, or I am unfamiliar with the background of the passage. My co-worker would be able to help me, explain what the passage means to him/her. A while back we had read over 1 Corinthians 13:4-7, it talks about the different characteristics of Love. And now since that group of people have read that passage together. When we see each other, we can remind each other and see how we are doing trying to achieve that perfect love God calls us to. It creates common ground for all of us and allows some sort of accountability among us.

One time I was in the lunchroom, minding my own business and I noticed one of the girls reading her Bible. Now that was pretty cool. I have to tell you the truth; I was chicken at first to say anything. So I waited till later in the day when there was no one else around and asked her about it. And sure enough she told me boldly that she believed in Jesus and was living her life for Him. And I can tell you that we will email each other and ask how God is working in our lives along with any prayer requests. Those days that I see her or get an email from her are just so great. They are so encouraging. God has totally blessed me through this. It is kind of amazing that I was scared at first to say anything. But you know what God gave me the words to speak and He took care of me. Why was I so scared then? It is kind of frightening to think about all the other relationships that I have missed out on because I was scared and didn't take that step of faith.

I believe there is a lot of power in keeping each other accountable. Why not have an accountability partner or partners at work. If you figure you work for the same company, both of you are familiar with what is going on and the struggles within the company. You both can relate to the stresses and conditions of the job. Let's say you are having a rough day; this might allow you to walk down the hallway and talk to your brother or sister in Christ and be encouraged by them. I know that time is a precious asset in all of our lives. So it might be hard to get together. But set aside a time, maybe every Friday maybe you get together with a group and spend a little time reading in the scriptures, praying for the company and each other, and checking to make sure everyone is doing okay. Do it over lunch. We need to watch out for each other: "Be self-controlled and alert. Your enemy the devil prowls around like a roaring lion looking for someone to devour. Resist him, standing firm in the faith, because you know that your brothers throughout the world are undergoing the same kind of sufferings" (1 Peter 5:8-9). So if we know we are being prayed upon, let's do it together, lets resist the devil together. God says we can have partners, we can work as a team. "Brothers, if someone is caught in a sin, you who are spiritual should restore him gently. But watch yourself, or you also maybe tempted. Carry each other's burdens, and in this way you will fulfill the law of Christ" (Galatians 6:1-2). Paul tells us that we should carry each other's burdens. It's not always fun and easy, but to our brothers and sisters in Christ we have that responsibility. Maybe we have experienced that burden before: divorce, depression, lust, someone close to us passing away, loss of job. We can help that next person to go through that. We can share with them our mistakes so they will not do the same. Even more importantly share with them what helped you through those situations.

There are two things that have to happen. First we have to let our pride go. We can't lie to ourselves that we can do everything ourselves. Also we have to get over thinking that our time is much to valuable to set aside time to hear about what is going on in other people's lives. Especially if you are someone in upper management and you might go out with some people from the mailroom or a secretary. People might give you a hard time for that for spending time with someone in a lower corporate status. But if we are all believers we are suppose to look out for one another. Second we have to open up to one another. This may put ourselves in a vulnerable position. But I believe that God can use us when we are vulnerable. I also respect that something work related might not be able to be shared with everyone, and everyone should respect that. You should not use this to try to get a leg up or take advantage of anyone and vice versa.

In college two of my roommates and I had formed an accountability group, we ended up meeting once a week.

We set aside between an hour to hour and half just to meet and talk about what God is doing in our lives. We used that time as a spiritual check up. We asked each other a variety of questions throughout that time. Have we spent time in the word during this past week, and what has God taught you? How has your prayer life been, have there been any answers to prayer. Have we been good Stewarts of money, at least the little money that we had? Have we honored God with our thought life, is lust a problem? And all of us being students we had that common understanding about mid-term weeks, we understood the stress of those big papers, the lust factor, etc. So we would ask how school was going and we checked to make sure we were spending time with God and not just school. But here we were three twenty something guys, all in a secular college setting, wanting to live our lives for Christ. We had a lot in common and were able to encourage one another. We were experiencing a lot of the same pressures, struggles, and temptations. We were able to work them out together as a team.

I really think that God can use this to further His kingdom. Not only will we encourage and be encouraged by our brothers and sisters. It will also be a good witnessing aspect. Let us not underestimate the importance and the power of gathering with our brothers and sisters. "Let us not give up meeting together, as some are in the habit of doing, but let us encourage one another – and all the more as you see the Day approaching" (Hebrews 10:25).

Using Our
Time Wisely

*"Be very careful, then, how you live – not as
unwise but as wise, making the most of every
opportunity, because the days are evil".*

Ephesians 5:15

There are a lot of things that demand our time. It seems like we could never work enough to get caught up. There is always something that we can be doing more. There is always a certain show or game that we want to watch. I am very guilty with this one; I love the fall and watching football Sundays after church. I literally rush out of church so I don't miss any of the game. So then I would go spend three hours in front of a TV.

At work we always wished that we could have been the 'lucky' one and been born into money. We thought that if this was true it would solve all of our problems. The thing with time is different. Everyone whether they are multi-billionaires or a homeless person, we all have 24 hours in a day. No one is special and is able to have more or less time.

In the Psalms God warns us that our time is short here on earth. "Each man's life is but a breath. Man is a mere phantom as he goes to and fro: He bustles about, but only in vain" (Psalm 39:5-6). God is telling us in that our lives on earth is nothing compared to eternity, we are but a breath. If you think about that, how many times you take a breath a day, a year, a lifetime.

Since our lives are so short, we have to make a major impact while we are here. It doesn't even have to be major in the world's perspective. I think that in business we get caught up in numbers. God is not necessarily interested just in numbers. Some He has called us to reach thousands of people, like a Billy Graham. But He has called some of us just to teach Sunday morning Sunday school or to help out in dramas or in a nursing home. God has plans for us all to reach different people. "Be very careful, then, how you live – not as unwise but as wise, making the most of every opportunity, because the days are evil. Therefore do not be foolish, but understand what the Lord's will is" (Ephesians 5:15-17). And according to John we know that the devil has intentions to steal us from God. "The thief comes only to steal and kill and destroy; I (Jesus) have come that they may have life, and have it to the full" (John 10:10). That is why the days are evil, because of the devil. That's why Bible is such a great reminder, "Therefore, as we have opportunity, let us do good to all people, especially to those who belong to the family of believers" (Galatians 6:10). This is also a reminder that our fellow brothers and sisters in Christ also need encouragement, and we should not take those opportunities for granted. Sometimes we over look each other and forget that our brothers and sisters in Christ can hurt and maybe struggling spiritually at times. Sometimes we feel that we won't have any impact on another believer or non-believer for that fact. We need to get over that mindset and encourage each other from time to time. Once again we have to step out in faith and speak those words of encouragement.

If you are in a sharing opportunity you might be the last Christian that comes in contact with a non-believer. I have heard stories where because people say hi to complete strangers, or even by giving friends a call on the phone have saved their lives. The other person was feeling down and that no one cared about them, so they were going to take their own lives. That is the devil lying to these people that they are worthless.

"Be diligent in these matters; give yourself wholly to them, so that everyone may see your progress" (1 Timothy 4:15). Basically God is telling us if we are going to do something, do it with everything we got. We might never have that opportunity ever again. We can look at Esther. It is a beautiful Old Testament story about how God placed Esther to save the whole Jewish population. This is the cliff note version, which the whole story is much better and I really encourage you to read the whole story. Esther basically won a beauty contest and was chosen to be queen. What the king didn't know was she was Jewish. The king's right hand man, Haman, had a plot to kill all of the Jewish people. However Esther was able to talk to the king and convince him not to kill the Jewish people, instead Haman was hanged. God did his work by placing people in position to save his people. Then it was up to those people God had placed in that situation, they have to take that step of faith. If Esther decided not to do anything, if she decided just to take a step back and watch, she would have seen her family die, friends, and all of her ancestors. "And who knows but that you have come to royal position for such a time as this" (Esther 4:14)? Are we sitting back and letting opportunities pass us by. Yes God might not be calling us to royalty, but he has specific plans for us, and they are just as important as Esther's was.

So let us not watch our days and hours pass us by. Let's be proactive in our lives. Instead of watching movie after movie, let's let God write our own movie for us starring you. Let's go out and make a difference for Christ.

Power of
Slowing Down

"Be still, and know that I am God".

Psalm 46:10

We live in a very busy world. People are always on the go; they have meetings to go to, or taking the kids to football practice, etc. It is very easy to get caught up in everything; there is just so much going on. When I first started working I was told that I should try to get involved as much as I could. It is a great way to network, to learn about the community and the organization. And that's true. There are a lot of people that take that route. Sure these people probably get recognized and will probably move up the corporate ladder faster than those who don't. But it is not just simply their time that they are giving up. It also takes tolls on their families, friends, and relationships. These as we have discussed earlier you can't put a price tag on. It is something that both parties have to work on and make an investment in. And some people are totally fine with not spending hours with their kids or spouse.

However, God is not like that though. "Be still, and know that I am God" (Psalm 46:10). That is pretty simple. Sometimes we know that God is God but we really don't know it. For instance we know that our kids want more time with us, but we still don't give them that time. We still spend sixty hours at the office. We justify it by saying that we are going to provide better for them, and that this is just temporary and tomorrow will be different. Well remember this that tomorrow never comes. We are also warned: "We hear that some among you are idle. They are not busy; they are busybodies" (2 Thessalonians 3:11). Let us use our time wisely. God wants some quality time with us. I encourage you just spending fifteen minutes with God; it can make a world of difference. And after a while just increase that fifteen minutes a couple of minutes each week or every couple of days.

Sometimes those fifteen minutes might just be spent reading God's word. And don't just read it to say you read it. Just read a little bit and soak it in. I have been told that you don't hurry up and eat a nice steak; no you take your time and enjoy it. Same with God's word don't read it like a newspaper. What I have found to help is finding a regular time to read the Bible. Some people like to do it when they get up or right before they go to bed, or if they have time at lunch, whatever works for you. I personally like to do it in the morning, that way I can dwell on the passage that I read throughout the day.

If you struggle with getting into God's word I have a couple of suggestions. The first one is find someone else who has a desire to read the Bible. Then the two or three of you could read that same passage, maybe you would both start in the gospel of Matthew and work your way through the New Testament. And lets say once a week you then could talk about what you have read, kind of like an accountability partner. It's kind of like someone to go to the gym with. You want to go workout but usually things seem to pop up. But if you have someone to meet you at the gym you tend to go a little more often. And you're glad that you went because you feel great afterwards. The second suggestion is buying a new Bible. It sounds kind of foolish but sometimes when you buy new things you get excited about them. So that might just be the spark that you need. Also this will allow you to get a Bible that you like. So many Bibles now they come with study notes, dictionaries, and concordances, which help you to understand more what you are reading. The third suggestion involves another purchase, and that is buying the Bible on tape or CD. That way you could listen to it on the way to work or while you are working. If you go this route I encourage you also to dig into your own Bible. Get to know it inside and out. But again this might be a way to spark an interest into reading. In all reality I think it comes down to discipline and a desire just to read and dive into God's word. I am trying to get into the word just about daily. But sometimes it is more of a routine; sometimes it is a cheeseburger, when it needs to be a nice big juicy steak.

Another way you might spend those fifteen minutes is praying. I encourage you to develop a "hit list." Maybe it is only five specific things that you would like to see God do in your life and the people around you. Maybe your hit list would consist of time that you could spend with a fellow co-worker; it could be prayer for your healing, or your children, your spouse. You could also spend that time in worship. The problem that I have grasping is that God wants quality time.

"Be still before the Lord and wait patiently for him; do not fret when men succeed in their ways when they carry out their wicked schemes. Refrain from anger and turn from wrath; do not fret – it leads only to evil. For evil men will be cut off, but those who hope in the Lord will inherit the land" (Psalm 37:7-9). Again the Lord commands us to turn to him and focus on him. God doesn't care what everyone else is doing. I think that some of us, myself included. We are always looking around to see what everyone else is doing. Why are we so concerned about how people are going to accept us? "We probably wouldn't worry about what people think of us if we could know how seldom they do," Olin Miller. Again we live in a very busy and always moving world. I struggle with not moving and doing something. Which causes me to struggle with being still before the Lord. But you know what I have personally found to be helpful is finding a spot to get away. Now this spot I don't bring a cell phone or a beeper, it is away from a TV and radio. Try to limit the distractions; of course each person has different distractions in their lives. The place that I found to get away from these distractions were going for walks in the park. It also helped me to realize God's beauty. I know that it kind of sounds cheesy but I hear the birds, I see the green grass with the flowers. "But Jesus often withdrew to lonely places and prayed" (Luke 5:16). So if it was important for Jesus I am sure that it will be worthwhile for us also. In Luke it mentioned lonely, according to Webster's dictionary lonely is "standing apart from others of its kind; isolated; alone; solitary."[xi] And that is true; it is not always easy and not always super exciting. But I think that it is something that if we are consistent that God can really work through that time and change our lives. Give it a try; what do you have to lose.

Let us always remember that God reminds us to "Come near to God and he will come near to you" (James 4:8). God is just waiting on us to make the next move. He created us; He gave us his one and only Son, through which we are redeemed. He desires to have a relationship with us. And since God wants it to be genuine relationship with us, He gave us free will. He gave us the chance to decide. Just remember the parable of the Lost Son in Luke.

"Jesus continued: 'there was a man who had two sons. The younger one said to his father, 'Father, give me my share of the estate.' So he divided his property between them. 'Not long after that, the younger son got together all he had, set off for a distant country and there squandered his wealth in wild living. After he had spent everything, there was a severe famine in that whole country, and he began to be in need. So he went and hired himself out to a citizen of that country, who sent him to his fields to feed pigs. He longed to fill his stomach with the pods that the pigs were eating, but no one gave him anything. When he came to his senses, he said, 'How many of my father's hired men have food to spare, and here I am starving to death! I will set out and go back to my father and say to him: Father, I have sinned against heaven and against you. I am no longer worthy to be called your son; make me like one of your hired men. So he got up and went to his father. But while he was still a long way off, his father saw him and was filled with compassion for him; he ran to his son, threw his arms around him and kissed him. The son said to him, 'father, I have sinned against heaven and against you. I am no longer worthy to be called your son. But the father said to his servants, 'quick bring the best robe and put it on him. Put a ring on his finger and sandals on his feet. Bring the fattened calf and kill it. Let's have a feast and celebrate. For this son of mine was dead and is alive again; he was lost and is found.' So they began to celebrate" (Luke 15:11-24).

How would you feel if your children came to you and asked for half of their inheritance whiled you were still alive? I know that it would not go to good with my parents. Especially if they knew I was going to Las Vegas with all my money to gamble it all away. This father in the parable seemed pretty reasonable. First off he gave the son his wish, his part of the inheritance. I am sure that it disappointed him, but he knew to have his son's love he had to give him his freedom. What totally blows me away is when we read that from far off the Father saw his son from a distance and ran out to him, and he had compassion. I know that I personally would have problems, I probably would have been more like the second son. Fortunate for us God is just like that Father in the story. He is waiting and looking out for us. Everyday He is looking and waiting for us to come back to Him, He doesn't care where we have been or what we have done. He is just happy that we are home and spending time with Him.

Let's be Extreme

"Just then his disciples returned and were surprised to find him talking with a woman. But no one asked, 'What do you want?' or 'Why are you talking with her?'".

John 4:27

So what is being an extreme disciple of Christ? What does it look like, what do these people do? We hear this word extreme a lot these days. We have extreme sports, along with extreme car chases. What is this word extreme? According to Webster's Dictionary extreme is defined as the following: "in or to the greatest degree; to an excessive degree; far from what is normal."[xii] Can you think of the last extreme thing you have done? Personally I can't, especially when you compare my life to people jumping out of planes and bungee jumping.

Let's look at a couple of stories in the Bible where people were extreme. First off we will look at Peter. "During the fourth watch of the night Jesus went out to them, walking on the lake. When the disciples saw him walking on the lake, they were terrified. 'It's a ghost,' they said, and cried out in fear. But Jesus immediately said to them: 'Take courage!' It is I. Don't be afraid.' 'Lord, if it's you,' Peter replied ' tell me to come to you on the water.' 'Come,' he said. Then Peter got down out of the boat, walked on the water and came toward Jesus" (Matthew 14:25-29). To me Peter did a pretty extreme thing here. Peter was walking on water, doing the impossible. One thing here Peter displayed was faith. At least at first, later on in the passage Jesus reached out and caught Peter since he began to sink. And I think that is just the thing. If we do something extreme like Peter. It first takes faith to do, but we have to continue on having faith in God that He will provide for us and take care of us. And in this passage Peter lacked that, not saying I don't blame Peter. I know that I am in the same boat, something comes up which makes me think about what I am doing and then I realize that I am not suppose to be doing this and I tend to doubt them. Again the same with Peter. He realizes that this is amazing that he is walking on water, this is something he physically shouldn't be doing, but Peter is doing it. Then he sees some wind coming and he was scared. Which then he started to lose faith.

How about a second instance in the Bible: "When a Samaritan woman came to draw water, Jesus said to her, 'Will you give me a drink?' (His disciples had gone into the town to buy food.) The Samaritan woman said to him, 'You are a Jew and I am a Samaritan woman. How can you ask me for a drink?' (For Jews do not associate with Samaritans.) Jesus answered her, 'If you knew the gift of God and who it is that asks you for a drink, you would have asked him and he would have given you living water.' 'Sir,' the woman said, 'you have nothing to draw with and the well is deep. Where can you get this living water? Are you greater than our father Jacob, who gave us the well and drank from it himself, as did also his sons and his flocks and herds?' Jesus answered, 'Everyone who drinks this water will be thirsty again, but whoever drinks the water I give him will never thirst. Indeed, the water I give him will become in him a spring of water welling up to eternal life" (John 4:7-14). Jesus just did one extreme thing after another. By studying the gospels we can learn from Him. Here in this scripture passage Jesus goes out on a limb and talks to someone that is socially un-acceptable. This was politically incorrect what Jesus did. And the woman reminded Jesus about this. And if we read more of the story we are told: "Just then his disciples returned and were surprised to find him talking with a woman. But no one asked, 'What do you want?' or 'Why are you talking with her'" (John 27)? However Jesus continued to converse with her and didn't let her off easy. Later on in the passage Jesus begins talking about her problems with not having a husband and living with some guy. Jesus didn't care about what people thought about Him. He was willing to go out on a limb. Therefore since He did the woman gathered people from the town and they believed in Christ. "Many of the Samaritans from that town believed in him because of the woman's testimony" (John 4:39). Are we willing to go out on a limb like that? Are we willing to eat lunch with some-one we notice always eats by themselves. Or are we willing to sit by someone on the train instead of talking to ourselves and putting on headphones.

We need to step out of our comfort zone. That is the basic building block of doing something extreme. It is asking those tough questions and not settling for those common answers. It is challenging someone to change. We have to take that step of faith.

I don't think that in order for us to be extreme in our faith that we always have quit our jobs and become missionaries in a third world country. We can become extreme by just giving of our time. We can volunteer at a local hospital, or help teach Sunday school. We can be extreme by talking with people we don't usually talk to whether they are people of different races or social status. We don't always have to be doing the sky diving stuff. We just have to pray that God will give us opportunities to be extreme. And then when we receive those opportunities we have to be faithful and follow through with them. Sure before we take that leap and become extreme we might have those butterflies in our stomach. And that is when we just have to stop thinking about it. Take a look around, smile real big, and dive in headfirst.

Conclusion

"Let us fix our eyes on Jesus, the author and perfecter of our faith, who for the joy set before him endured the cross, scorning its shame, and sat down at the right hand of the throne of God".

Hebrews 12:2

First off I hope that you have found this helpful and worth your while. I know that God has blessed me along the way. It has given me a great deal of excitement. It has helped me just to go to God's word and see what He has to say. I know that probably most of it was review, and stuff you have heard before. Sometimes I think that is good, we need a refresher every once in a while. Also I feel that sometimes things are so obvious and people over look those things, until someone mentions the 'obvious.' And I hope that you dig into God's word to check with everything that you have read.

I once again just want to mention that I don't claim to know everything. And I am sure that we could go into a lot more depth on these topics that were touched upon. Which there are lots of other good books, along with the Bible that we can dig into to further our understandings and longings for Christ. The main thing is just knowing Jesus Christ personally as my Lord and Savior and trying to live my life for him day in and day out.

I just want to end with a couple of last words and especially some verses to encourage us. It is not an easy life. "In fact, everyone who wants to live a godly life in Christ Jesus will be persecuted" (2 Timothy 3:12). Which is not so encouraging, however in Romans we are told: "As the Scripture says, 'Anyone who trusts in him will never be put to shame'" (Romans 10:11). I guarantee that all of the hardships and persecution will be worth it. The Lord is not going to lead us on. God doesn't play those games. He is not setting us up for failure. Of course we will go through some valleys, but those really are great times of growth for us. There are some times that we take our focus off of Him and then our steps might become a little shaky. Let us also not forget our grand prize, spending eternity with our Savior and King, Jesus Christ.

"Being confident of this, that he who began a good work in you will carry it on to completion until the day of Christ Jesus" (Philippians 1:6). I know that we experience sometimes that we feel that God is so far away from us and he doesn't care about us. But that is a bunch of hogwash. He cares for us more than we ever know. Here in Philippians it tells us that He is not going to walk away from us. He gave us His son; He has been using people to invest in us. He is not simply going to walk away from us. He wants to see us grow and live for Him. "And my God will meet all your needs according to his glorious riches in Christ Jesus" (Philippians 4:19).

We can't fail if we give God the reigns of our lives. We will truly experience life if we give everything to God. Just think of the people that you could meet, the impact you could have on your community or even the country. "The Lord is with me; I will not be afraid. What can man do to me? The Lord is with me; he is my helper. I will look in triumph on my enemies" (Psalm 118:6-7). We have to get past the things that we see. "I tell you, my friends, do not be afraid of those who kill the body and after that can do no more. But I will show you whom you should fear: Fear him who, after the killing of the body, has the power to throw you into hell. Yes I tell you, fear him" (Luke 12:4-5). Of course our death is kind of a scary thing, but Luke is right. If we are living our lives for Christ we should have nothing to worry about. That is when we really start living our lives.

For some encouragement we can look at Job, where he lost everything but he still praises God. Listen to this: "While he was still speaking, yet another messenger came and said, 'Your sons and daughters were feasting and drinking wine at the oldest brother's house, when suddenly a mighty wind swept in from the desert and struck the four corners of the house. It collapsed on them and they are dead, and I am the only one who has escaped to tell you!' At this, Job got up and tore his robe and shaved his head. Then he fell to the ground in worship and said: 'Naked I came from my mother's womb, and naked I will depart. The Lord gave and the Lord has taken away; may the name of the Lord be praised.' In all this, Job did not sin by charging God with wrongdoing" (Job 1:18-22). Here Job loses his livestock, servants, and his own children, yet he does not sin or blame God. He still praises God through all that hardship. He was focused. "Life brings sorrows and joys alike. It is what a man does with them. Not what they do to him. That is a test of his mettle," Teddy Roosevelt. What are we doing with the sorrows and joys of our lives, are we letting the sorrows control our lives? Or we could look at Joseph again. His brothers sold him into slavery, he also ended up in prison. Then he was the king's right hand man, and helped saved a nation. He even saved his own family that sold him into slavery during the serve famine. And this is what Joseph tells his brothers: "Then Joseph said to his brothers, 'come close to me.' When they had done so, he said, 'I am your brother Joseph, the one you sold into Egypt! And now, do not be distressed and do not be angry with yourselves for selling me here, because I was to save lives that God sent me ahead of you. For two years now there has been famine in the land, and for the next five years there will not be plowing and reaping. But God sent me ahead of you to preserve for you a remnant on earth and to save your lives by a great deliverance'" (Genesis 45:4-7). All because Joseph didn't fold when things got hard, he kept on going. It is a great story, I really encourage you to read it and you can find it in Genesis 37-47. Lets not be so quick to give up on the Lord and his plans for us. "And we know that in all things God works for the good of those who love him, who have been called according to his purpose" (Romans 8:28).

"Therefore, since we are surrounded by such a great cloud of witnesses, let us throw off everything that hinders and the sin that so easily entangles, and let us run with perseverance the race marked out for us. Let us fix our eyes on Jesus, the author and perfecter of our faith, who for the joy set before him endured the cross, scorning its shame, and sat down at the right hand of the throne of God" (Hebrews 12:1-2). Let us break out of our routines and the ungodly things that consume us. And let's turn to Jesus. Let's let him write a great story, starring us as the lead. It gets boring watching someone else; God has His own great story for us. Let's live our lives to the fullest so we don't have to wonder and play those "what if" games.

Notes

i   Mead, Frank S. <u>12,000 Religious Quotations</u>. Grand Rapids, Michigan: Baker Book House, 1989

ii Mead, Frank S. <u>12,000 Religious Quotations</u>. Grand Rapids, Michigan: Baker Book House, 1989

iii Mead, Frank S. <u>12,000 Religious Quotations</u>. Grand Rapids, Michigan: Baker Book House, 1989

iv Mullins, Rich. <u>Songs</u>. Reunion Records

v   Mead, Frank S. <u>12,000 Religious Quotations</u>. Grand Rapids, Michigan: Baker Book House, 1989

vi Mead, Frank S. <u>12,000 Religious Quotations</u>. Grand Rapids, Michigan: Baker Book House, 1989

vii Griffiths, Michael, <u>Grace - Gifts (Developing What God has given the Church)</u>. William B. Ecrdmans Publishing Company. Grand Rapids. 1970

viii Strope, Leigh, <u>"Most workers lack retirement accounts"</u> Chicago Sun-Times. Saturday December 14, 2002

ix Strope, Leigh, <u>"Most workers lack retirement accounts"</u> Chicago Sun-Times. Saturday December 14, 2002

x   Webster's New World College Dictionary. Third Edition. 1997

xi   Webster's New World College Dictionary. Third Edition. 1997

xii   Webster's New World College Dictionary. Third Edition. 1997

Printed in the United States
19073LVS00001B/135